Morning by Morning

An African-American Devotional

Morning by Morning

An African-American Devotional

Edited by
Reverend Ronald S. Bonner

BET Publications, LLC
http://www.bet.com

NEW SPIRIT BOOKS are published by

BET Publications, LLC
c/o BET BOOKS
One BET Plaza
1900 W Place NE
Washington, DC 20018-1211

All Kensington Titles, Imprints, and Distributed Lines are available at special quantity dis-
counts for bulk purchases for sales promotions, premiums, fund-raising, and educational or
institutional use. Special book excerpts or customized printings can also be created to fit specific needs. For details, write or phone the office of the Kensington special sales manager:
Kensington Publishing Corp., 850 Third Avenue, New York, NY 10022, attn: Special Sales
Department, Phone: 1-800-221-2647.

ISBN: 1-58314-597-4

First Printing: January 2005
10 9 8 7 6 5 4 3 2 1

Printed in the United States of America

Foreword

The word of God teaches over and over again that prayer is the most powerful weapon in a believer's arsenal. From the awesome challenge that God gives in 2 Chronicles 7:14 through the words of Jesus encouraging us to "always pray," the biblical principle of the importance of prayer is quite clear.

God says in the Old Testament that if we humble ourselves and pray, God will hear us from heaven, forgive our sins, and heal the land. Jesus says that if we ask what we need in God's name, if it is in accord with the will of God, it will be done!

These biblical principles come alive in a very different way in the African-American experience. Both James Washington, in his *Conversations with God*, and Harold Carter, in his *The Prayer Tradition of Black People*, discuss these differences and the powerful way that black "prayer life" has made a difference. Theology is never impersonal, and theological is never "universal." Theology is culture-specific and is always done through the lenses of those who experience God and encounter God in their particularity. It is this theology that has shaped African-American prayer for more than 300 years.

The uniqueness of the African-American experience does not need rehearsing. Five hundred years of white supremacy have shaped the perspectives of Africans on this continent and Africans who live in the diaspora.

A personal encounter with Jesus Christ, however, has produced a theology and an understanding of prayer that is distinctly unique and breathtakingly inspiring! That is what you will experience in this volume. The writers who contribute to this devotional book have come to know God as the sons and daughters of Africa. That means that their forebears have known the middle passage, white supremacy, racism, segregation, Jim Crow, and the insanity of the "Ham Doctrine."

Through it all, however, the personal relationships that were developed by each of these writers' foreparents and the personal relationship that they have developed with Jesus Christ, have given them not only a different perspective on prayer—they also have a hope that is indestructible!

Their experience of prayer is quite personal. In Howard Thurman's autobiography, *With Head and Heart*, there is a clue to what follows in the devotional. The writers in this volume have a perspective on prayer that is shaped by both head and heart. These writers know Jesus for themselves and they also know what it means to be black in America! They know the risen Lord and they serve him.

At the same time, however, they have lived through the Civil Rights movement and have seen the hatred of white Christians who believe that the sons of Canaan were supposed to be "hewers of wood and drawers of water." They have lived in the 20th century—a century that Dr. Martin Luther King Jr. described as the most "segregated hour in America!" King also made reference to the eleven o'clock worship hour on Sunday mornings when white-racist Christians thought themselves superior to blacks and forced the creation of the African-American churches.

Because there flows through these writers' veins the blood of Harriet Tubman, Bishop Henry McNeal Turner, Edward Wilmot Blyden, Jarena Lee, Sojourner Truth, Marcus Garvey, and Queen Nzinga, they have a different hermeneutic. Their understanding of "calling on the Lord" to get an answer is a far different understanding than one that was shaped in the drawing rooms of Europe or in the cold, sterile halls of academia in New England in America. The whip, the auction block, the slave patrols, the fire hoses, the German shepherds, the overseers and the "Uncle Toms" have shaped the faith of these writers, and it bleeds through very powerfully as they speak of prayer from a very personal, powerful, and painful experience!

The same Jesus who met Africans in the holds of slave ships and in the cane breaks of Mississippi during slavery meets us today. That is the perspective they bring to their meditations, and that is why this volume goes straight to the heart of those of us who know personally the "stony road" that we have trod.

The writers in these pages use images and vignettes of experience from the African-American reality. Because they are like Ezekiel, who sat where his people sat, their meditations will certainly hit home among African-American readers. For readers of this devotional who are not African-American, their writings are just as important. They are important because they will give to the non-African-American audience a glimpse of a people whose faith could not be destroyed no matter how "bitter" the chastening rod. It will give the uninitiated a peek at the "glossary" and the "code language" of those who have known sorrow but who have come out of "the gloomy past" victoriously!

In the words of one of the writers in this volume and in the words of a gospel song, it will help the uninitiated reader to understand why African-Americans are so jubilant when they say, "We are still here!" I commend this volume to you, and I also commend the Christ who makes us more than conquerors to you. As you read this work, may God bless your reading with God's power and God's Spirit.

Jeremiah A. Wright Jr.
Trinity United Church of Christ
Chicago, Illinois

Introduction

I would like to thank you for choosing this volume and adding it to your collection of devotional materials. I trust that you will come to find this an indispensable tool for your daily praise life. Using this book as it is designed will help you develop your spiritual dexterity and strength. I know that while I was editing this resource I was getting stronger as I was being filled with God's word. Once you start reading *Morning by Morning*, please resist trying to read ahead. If you want more to read, then read the entire Bible chapter that each day's reflection is based on. In fact, as you progress, our hope is that reading the Bible alongside this devotional will become part of your daily devotional period.

Next, try to write a few notes each day as you reflect on what you have read. Think about how God is working in your life and write down your thoughts. Ask yourself how to apply today's lesson to your life. Then sing and fill your spirit with a Holy song, one based on God's redeeming love for you.

And now, beloved, please know the grace of God that comes through the love and sacrifice of our Lord and Savior Jesus Christ. May you grow in God as you exercise your faith daily, and may your works be blessed by God. In Jesus' name. Amen.

Ronald S. Bonner
Augsburg Fortress, Publishers

God Is Jealous

*"For you shall worship no other god, for the Lord, whose
name is Jealous, is a jealous God."*
EXODUS 34:14

Today's Prayer

Jealous is your name, oh God, and completely yours will I be. Oh
God even in your jealousy your love for us is evident. God because
you have been so good to me, I will give myself totally to your care
and instruction. Help me, God, be as true to you as you have been to
me. Amen.

Today's Reflection

God has every right to be jealous. God made us, has redeemed us,
sustains us, provides for us, and helps us sometimes even before we
are aware that we need help. However, God's jealousy is not out of
self-doubt or insecurity like our jealousy. God wants us to live full
and joyous lives and God knows that we will only be disappointed if
we stray away. So beloved, know God, serve God, and live in the joy
of life that our loving yet jealous God has for us.

My Prayer for Today:

To devote my thoughts and heart
to God, and to serve him and not
others + material things

Day 2

A Different Destination

"You led your people like a flock by the hand of Moses and Aaron."

PSALM 77:20

Today's Prayer

I need you to see me through the wilderness of this day as you saw your people through. Lead me by your Word as you led Moses and Aaron. Forgive me for my errors and help me reach my place of peace and comfort. Amen.

Today's Reflection

Moses and Aaron were faithful servants of God. However, they were flawed and gave in to their anger and sometimes followed the crowd when they should have followed God. Still God used them to serve God and to serve the people. They were men in God's service, yet they did not take the children over into the Promised Land. Sometimes in life we will not get all that we hope for. Our paths may differ, our destinations may be different, our earthly task may not be fulfilled, but as long as we stay true to God we have an assurance that where we go is where God wants us to be.

My Prayer for Today:

Lord, help me stay true to you. Do not let me lose myself and my purpose while I'm here. Help me to further serve you

Morning by Morning

Day 3

Take Heart

"The Lord said to him, 'This is the land I promised . . . but you will not cross over there.'"

DEUTERONOMY 34:4

Today's Prayer

God please give me the love for you that you bestowed upon Moses. Lord I want to love you that even in my most serious disappointment my love and obedience for you is strong. Help me to see the positive side to life and in each situation may I see how to give you thanks. Help me see with Moses' eyes. Amen.

Today's Reflection

Have you ever worked hard on a project only to see the reward or credit go to someone else? Were you angry, upset, did you plan to quit your job in protest? Well, consider Moses and his trip up Mount Nebo. God takes him up there and shows him the Promised Land and then tells him he will not cross over into it. Moses, I loved the work you did on that proposal and the way you worked with the client was fantastic but we have decided to give . . . the account. Steamed, disappointed? I'm sure you were and I'm sure Moses was as well; come on, Moses faced Pharaoh, the Red Sea, and had to put up with grumbling people for over 40 years. So take heart, beloved, stay faithful, for every Moses-type situation that comes to a disappointing end may be the beginning that prepares you for a Joshua opportunity.

My Prayer for Today:

Lord, allow me to be grateful for what you have given me. Help me realize that in my disappointments, there are blessings. Where a door closes a window opens

God's Glory

"He is the reflection of God's glory and the exact imprint of God's very being . . ."

HEBREWS 1:3

Today's Prayer

Gracious God who is the Creator of Life, may I bask in the sunlight of your love this day. May your glory be ever present with me and may I give you total praise this day. May all that I do give glory to you. Amen.

Today's Reflection

Jesus Christ for Christians is the Son of God who died for our sins in order for us to be forgiven for our sinfulness. Jesus had to be made a sacrifice for us because there was no other way. God in God's love for us demonstrated that love by offering up Jesus to be a sacrificial lamb whose blood was shed for our sins. Jesus became the Passover Lamb so the death angel will pass us by. It is a wonderful story, yet many people don't believe, even some who confess to be Christian. Nevertheless, Jesus made the ultimate sacrifice and obeyed God even unto death. What sacrifices are you willing to make to obey God? Take time out to give God praise and to give God the glory. Praise God, beloved, not just with your mouth today but also with your life. Help someone in need today and when they say thank you, have them give that praise to God.

My Prayer for Today:

Lord, help me to praise you with my mouth and actions. Help me to remember Jesus' sacrifice, and to make sacrifices in my life

Day 5

A Difficult Task

*"But the Lord said to him, 'Go, for he is an instrument
whom I have chosen to bring my name before Gentiles and
kings and before the people of Israel.'"*

ACTS 9:15

Today's Prayer

God, thank you for the changes that you have made in my heart
and in my understanding of you. Help me to be strong as I try to live
according to your will and not to the will of popular society or my
peers. Help me to follow you God now that you have brought such a
wonderful change to my life. Amen.

Today's Reflection

Imagine that God told you to be the personal escort to church of a
mass murderer who has been pardoned on a technicality. Well, imagine that is what Ananias was feeling. Has God ever given you a difficult task, one that involved you having to go against the grain, to go
against your peers; what about your boss? Sometimes taking a stand
for God means taking a stand with God, even against seemingly impossible odds. But beloved, God will not leave you alone if you do;
you like Ananias will hear God speak to you and you will find favor
with God. So go and do what God has called you to do.

My Prayer for Today:

*Lord, allow me to act according
to your will. Allow me the stance
for you and your teachings*

Morning by Morning

Day 6

New Hope

*"For God alone my soul waits in silence, for my hope is
from him."*

PSALM 62:5

Today's Prayer

Oh my soul when life gives me twists and turns and valley moments, may I be able to take comfort in knowing that God is with
me. Amen.

Today's Reflection

Have you ever driven north on I-24 from Atlanta to Nashville?
If so, you know that about 130 to 140 miles north of Atlanta you
will begin to ascend into the Smoky Mountains. The first time I
took that drive I was very uncertain of how I was going to fare.
Would there be a twist I wasn't prepared for, would I be in the
path of a runaway truck? Would my brakes or nerves give out?
However, the only thing I could do was pray to God and keep
moving. I made it and guess what, after the last truck grade and
turn of concern there before me was this beautiful panoramic
scene. Imagine the sun shining, the blue sky above, green trees
in the distance and a beautiful lake and river all in the same vision. And there on the bridge which is named for the river and
lake is the name of the city. "New Hope," I shouted. It seems that
after every difficult situation God provides a new hope for us. A
vision that lets us know how much God loves us. But then I
shouted again, because I realized that when I am going south on
I-24 God will give me a new hope to take me through the mountains that I am about to approach. So beloved please know that

whether you have come through something or you are getting ready to go through something, God has a new hope for you.

My Prayer for Today:

Day 7

When to Love

*"I am giving you these commands so that you may love one
another."*

JOHN 15:17

Today's Prayer

Loving God, help me to love others as I seek to love you and my-self. I need your help to be your witness of love. Amen.

Today's Reflection

Loving one another does not mean having sex with each other. However, that is how our society has viewed love, as sex. Consider all of the dating shows on television and all of the talk about who is in relationships with others. A popular song for the 70's suggested that if you can't be with your lover then a substitute would do. I had a chance to fully understand what Jesus meant. I was traveling and a man in the gas station could not pay for his gas. The song came to mind and so did Jesus' command, so I offered to pay for the man's gas. You see, if it was one of my sons in that situation I would gladly pay for their gas because I love them. But they were not there so I ap-plied that love to the person who was there. Outside, the man said thank you, Reverend. My act of love exposed my heart. Who can you show love to today and expose your heart?

My Prayer for Today:

Something Inside

"This is the Spirit of truth, whom the world cannot receive,
because it neither sees him nor knows him. You know him,
because he abides with you, and he will be in you."
JOHN 14:17

Today's Prayer

Gracious God, continue to lead me and guide me. Without you I find myself drifting away and being swayed by my desires. Help me, Lord, to live a holy and disciplined life in Christ. Amen.

Today's Reflection

A few years ago I watched a child play with her dessert. She took some cereal with a circular shape and pushed down into the mire of played-with-but-abandoned melting ice cream. After a few minutes the cereal popped back to the top of this mired concoction and spoke to me. Now I had heard the Rev. Freddie Haynes say that Shakespeare often got sonnets from stones, so I thought perhaps I could get a faith lesson from this fruity-looking cereal loop. So I invited the cereal to speak. It said that God's people and I should have something in common. You noticed that I was pushed down in a mire of mess but yet I popped back to the top. Don't you know that God's chosen should have something inside of them that keeps them from staying down? Beloved, God has placed within us the Holy Spirit, which is there to guide and comfort us. No matter how hard life gets, God is giving us something on the inside that will not let us stay down or defeated. Trust in God and you will always, no matter how far down you are, will always come back to the top.

My Prayer for Today: *Lead me & Guide me*

Day 9

False Intelligence

"Their idols are silver and gold, the work of human hands."
PSALM 115:4

Today's Prayer

Holy God, in today's world there are so many conflicting messages that sometimes I get confused. Loving God, open my eyes and ears to see and hear your truth. God I need you to speak clearly to me so I know what is real and not false. Amen.

Today's Reflection

Beloved do you know that idol worship is just that, idle worship? To worship idols can only lead to false understanding or intelligence. In other words, it is stupid and will leave you empty and alone. Don't get caught up with what is popular; instead hold fast to the principles of love that God commands us. It may not get you promoted to follow God, but you will be upheld by the Ancient of Days. Forget the false idols that will only lead to your demise. Serve God and you will have success in life that is solid and lasting.

My Prayer for Today:

Day 10

Praise God

"Bless the Lord, O my soul, and do not forget all his benefits."

PSALM 103:2

Today's Prayer

God, I want you to shine in me so that your light will cause my face to glow and reflect your love to all who see me. God, I love you and I want to stop and acknowledge how great you are. Loving God, thank you for being with me in life, thank you for the success that you have brought my way. Thank you God for not abandoning me when I left you. God, I seek each day to be the person you want me to be. God, I lift my hands and my heart to you; I will praise you all day long. Thank you, thank you, thank you, God, for all that you have done and all that you will do for me. Praise you for you alone, oh Holy God, are worthy of my praise. Amen.

Today's Reflection

In too many of our congregations we are being taught that if we praise God then God will bless us. We are told if we send up praise then God will rain down blessings upon us. So we act up in church thinking that we can manipulate God into doing our bidding. Beloved, that is not praise, that is a dangerous method that may give you a taste of hell's fire. Beloved, we are to worship God, however, not with an expectation that if we shout enough or send 1,000 emails that we can order God to bless us. Daughter, Son, God blesses us in spite of us because God loves us. We praise God in thankfulness for what God has already done for us. Praise God, beloved, with our lives, praise God by sharing with someone how God has made a difference in your life. Praise God every day, and sometimes use words; otherwise let your life be praise to God.

My Prayer for Today:

Morning by Morning

Day 11

One Thing

*"But, you, beloved, build yourselves up on your most holy
faith; pray in the Holy Spirit; keep yourselves in the love of
God; look forward to the mercy of our Lord Jesus Christ
that leads to eternal life."*
JUDE 1:20–21

Today's Prayer

Holy God, help me to grow in spiritual strength so I can stay faithful to you. Strengthen me Lord so I can help others to be strong in you as well. Amen.

Today's Reflection

Beloved, there are not many things that we have to do in life. There is really only one thing that we are required to do for God. Consider the moon, do you see it night after night hanging silently in the sky? What does the moon do; what is its purpose? The moon has one purpose and that is to reflect the sun. Beloved, as a Christian you only have one purpose as well and that is to reflect the Son. Yes, we are to reflect the Son of God, Jesus. Beloved, if you do that one thing day in and day out you will receive the promise of eternal life. What a reward for just doing one thing.

My Prayer for Today:

Day 12

Jesus

*"In the beginning was the Word, and the Word was with
God, and the Word was God."*

JOHN 1:1

Today's Prayer

Jesus, Jesus, Jesus, I love saying your name. Jesus, thank you for
your gift of sacrifice. I am unworthy, but because you loved me so
much I will make changes in my life to honor you. Help me to live in
a manner that reflects your love in my life. I love you, Jesus. Amen.

Today's Reflection

John is very clear in indicating that Jesus is divine. Not in some
earthly notion but divine in the sense that Jesus is God. And that
Jesus came to bring God's Word into our life. Jesus is the message of
God. And what is that message? That God loves you and desires the
best that life has to offer. God loves you to the point that God decided to pay your debts off without penalty and give you a new clean
slate. Jesus paid your debt to God with his life. Now friend, go in the
knowledge of God's love for you and live your life in the renewed
state that God has given you.

My Prayer for Today:

Who Knew?

"When the steward tasted the water now become wine, and did not know where it came from (though the servants who had drawn the water knew), the steward called the bridegroom."
JOHN 2:9

Today's Prayer

Gracious God, please change the water of life into wine, a wine that is better than anything I would have without your love in my life. God I need you, keep me faithful to you, don't let me become consumed by improper attitudes or desires. Let me be found tasteful to you. Amen.

Today's Reflection

Who knew? I love the fact that the servants who were doing what Jesus requested knew. Not the bridegroom, not the host of the wedding reception, not the featured guest, or the steward in charge of the feast knew what Jesus had done. Our society is like that sometimes: the big shots don't get it, but those who are faithful to God's Word, those who follow Jesus know. I often think about growing up wondering who knew that God would bless me with success in life. From ghetto streets to the halls of Corporate and now Religious America, God has brought me. Where has God brought you? Who knew? God knew. How marvelous are the works of God!

My Prayer for Today:

Day 14

Seek the Lord

*"Seek the Lord while he may be found, call upon him while
he is near."*

ISAIAH 55:6

Today's Prayer

Loving God who lets me go about my daily business, may I not in
my haste to satisfy my needs miss the chance to seek your counsel. I
know that I think I know everything, but Lord I need to hear from
you today. For lost I am without you. Come, Lord, I pray, incline
your ears to hear my prayers for your counsel. Amen.

Today's Reflection

We are often very excellent in obtaining the things that we want
for comfort. Sometimes we have a written or a mental checklist of
what we need to be considered successful, either to others or to ourselves. Sometimes we are so focused, because of our busy lives, that
we miss what God is telling us about true success. Beloved, do not
take God's love for you for granted. Take a moment to pause and invite God into all of the business that you have to conduct today. Seek
God's guidance in how you should handle today's tasks.

My Prayer for Today:

Day 15

Well-Fed But Misled

*"A Samaritan woman came to draw water and Jesus said
to her, 'Give me a drink.' "*
JOHN: 4:7

Today's Prayer

God I don't want to be fat on falsehood or delighted in decep-
tions. God I know that it is better to enter into your Realm hungry,
than to enter into hell on a full stomach. Search me for falseness and
remove it from me, let it burn away and not me. Amen.

Today's Reflection

The woman at the well was doing her chores and had the equip-
ment to do them. Jesus says to her, give me a drink. For this woman
had her dipping-in-the-well tools with her. Do you know anyone
who, whenever you see them, they have their dipping tools with
them? You know, their dipping-into-everybody's-business tools with
them? Whom do you know who is the source of rumors? When we
encounter Jesus, he points out that what he has to offer is better than
what we have. We should be like this woman and request to take
what Jesus has to offer. Once we are full on the Good News of Jesus,
simple gossip will no longer satisfy us. Go and share the good news
of Christ to others.

My Prayer for Today:

Day 16

Missing the Chance to Serve

*"But on the first day of the week, at early dawn, they came
to the tomb, taking the spices that they had prepared."*

LUKE 24:1

Today's Prayer

Thank you God for this day to serve you. Keep me from thinking
I can do my thing and that you will stand for it. Jesus be dynamic in
my life, helping me to attend to you even when it is not convenient
for me to do so. Amen.

Today's Reflection

These women were certain that they would find Jesus on Sunday
where he had been laid on Friday. Sometimes we want to put Jesus
on ice when we are trying to score that big deal or make a favorable
impression with a special someone. We want to lay our Jesus down
on Friday night, seal him in a tomb of weekend fun, and then go and
get him on Sunday in time for church. But friends, just like Jesus did
not lie still for these women whom he loved, he will not lie still for
you. Put Jesus first; don't worry about what is popular. Put Jesus first
and don't miss the opportunity to serve Jesus.

My Prayer for Today:

Day 17

Friendship Finds Faith

"Where you go, I will go."
RUTH 1:16b

Today's Prayer

Holy God, thank you for putting people in our lives who help us through difficult days and seasons. May we have a friend like Ruth, who when we are down and feeling blue will stick beside us and share our pain and sorrow, and help us realize our brighter tomorrow. Amen.

Today's Reflection

Naomi was feeling sorry for herself and with good reason. Naomi had lost what her society said was important for a woman to have, a husband and sons. Now she was all alone except for her daughters-in-law who seemingly were just as without means, as she was, whom she told to go home. However, Ruth had become more than a daughter-in-law; she had become Naomi's friend and would not leave her in this state of despair and loneliness. Do you know that God loves us like a best friend and will not forsake us when we feel lonely or blue? God will not even forsake us when we are feeling on top of the world and believe that we no longer have need for God. Friend, God is there for us no matter what. God offers a friendship that will help us find our faith and enrich it.

My Prayer for Today:

Do What Is Right

"The Lord said to Cain, 'Why are you angry and why has
your countenance fallen?'"

GENESIS 4:6

Today's Prayer

God may this day open my mind and my heart to not see labels. I
don't want to see as I have always seen, I want to see as you see. I
want to see people and not the labels that society and I have placed
on them. I don't want to view people with apathy or disgust or false
esteem, today I want to view them as subjects of your love and thus
I need to love them as well. Help me God not to see labels and to see
what is right in your sight, not mine. Amen.

Today's Reflection

All right, Cain, where is Abel? God says. I don't know is his
reply. Come on God, says Cain, am I responsible for him? God already
knew the answer and for some reason, disbelief in God's power I
suppose, Cain thought he could hide his sin from God. Most of us
carry some sin of separation from others within ourselves. We get
too high and mighty when good fortune shines on us and we begin
to forget others who have helped us along the way. Sometimes we
step over the person who can be a help to us in order to clamor for
the attention of someone we have come to idolize. Be careful that
we don't turn idolizing into idolatry; we must remember that God
is our creator and God alone we should worship. So think for a
moment, whom am I at odds with, not what would be the right
thing for me to do? Okay, make amends. Where's the phone?

My Prayer for Today:

Making God Sad

*"And the Lord was sorry that he had made humankind
on the earth, and it grieved him to his heart."*

GENESIS 6:6

Today's Prayer

Loving God, may this day be a day of your love throughout the world. Help me, God, to live a day that is pleasing to you. Help me to be a comfort to you and those I encounter, God. Thank you for loving me and may I display my thanks by how I show my love for others. Amen.

Today's Reflection

Just think, only six chapters into the Bible and God is so mad that God considers plans to destroy the world. What stopped God from going forward with this plan? How do we make God sad today? The Bible tells us that Noah found favor in God's sight; would we find that much favor in God's sight? Yeah, I know you heard that slogan about being favored, but are you to the point that God would have a change of heart because of you? And if yes, would you build an ark in the middle of a desert? We have much to think about when we talk about God's favor in our lives. Neither parroting slogans nor coming into some money is evidence that we are truly favored by God. When God shows favor on us, not only do we benefit but those around us do as well.

My Prayer for Today:

False Love

"How long, you people, shall my honor suffer shame? How long will you love vain words, and seek after lies?"

PSALM 4:2

Today's Prayer

Creator God, who has set before us the proper way to live and love, I ask that you will help me this day to move along the path that you designed especially for me. Help me to hear and heed your voice, help me to listen in the stillness for your roar. Amen.

Today's Reflection

We place demands on God and we expect God to respond to our demands as if the roles are reversed. In this short Psalm God speaks in a clear voice: "How long will you love delusions and seek false gods?" How long indeed will we go after false gods of immediate and cheap pleasure, how long will we love falsely? How long will we make our desires our god? Why do we chase after deluded love, that which leaves us empty and often hurting inside? God stands at the doorways of our hearts, waiting to come in and give us a real love based on trust and obedience. Beloved, obey God, and no matter how tempting, leave the delusions and false gods alone.

My Prayer for Today:

Compassion for the Road

"If I send them home hungry, they will faint on the way,
and some of them have come from a great distance."
MARK 8:3

Today's Prayer

God, as I travel back and forth today, let me forget about being on time and let me travel with compassion for others. Let me not look down on others, but give me a sense of what others are facing. Let me travel as part of a community, bringing a smile to give to someone who will need it for their journey. Amen.

Today's Reflection

Jesus is concerned about our entire being, not just the spiritual but also our physical being. That is why Jesus wanted to make sure the people here were fed real food. Yes, Jesus is aware that we are to be fed the Word of God, but he clearly knows that physical food for our physical bodies is also important. Jesus showed compassion and did not want to send these people away hungry. Each day we can show compassion for someone who is in need. If we open our hearts, we can see as Jesus sees when it comes to helping others.

My Prayer for Today:

Day 22

Seeing Through the Trickery

"But knowing their hypocrisy, he said to them, 'Why are you putting me to the test? Bring me a denarius and let me see it.' "

MARK 12:15

Today's Prayer

Gracious and loving God, I need help being consistent in how I serve you. I have really good days when I am caring and sharing but sometimes I get caught going against your will. I make mistakes; help me to see and to understand clearly when the evil comes to trick and trap me into saying or doing something that is against your will for my life. Amen.

Today's Reflection

Have you ever read the entire twelfth chapter of Mark in one reading? Gee, everywhere that Jesus turned someone was trying to trick him or trap him to say something questionable, so they could arrest him. But Jesus could see through their hypocrisy. Jesus could see through their well-meaning questions and see the evil that lurked behind. Beloved, take pause and know that when you take a stand for Christ the world will come after you as well, with well-wishers who are out to trap you. With God on your side you will be able to see through their hypocrisy as well. But here is a clue: don't get angry, that only cuts off blood to your brain; remain calm, say a quick God-help-me prayer, and respond with a cool question that they won't expect. Not only will you see through their hypocrisy, but also they will be exposed to everyone else around.

My Prayer for Today:

Day 23

God Will Make the Call

*"As indeed he says in Hosea, 'Those who were not my peo-
ple I will call "my people," and her who was not beloved I
will call "beloved." ' "*

ROMANS 9:25

Today's Prayer

God of Mercy, choose me to be on your side. I believe in you, I try each day to live in a manner that is pleasing to you. I have thrown off the garments of arrogance and pride that did fit me very well and have replaced them with garments of love and humility. Please God, choose me for your team. Amen.

Today's Reflection

Have you ever had to wait on the sidelines while the captains chose their teams? Well, I have. In football I was always a first choice, but for basketball I knew I had better say "next." I had skills and I was the fastest person in the neighborhood amongst my peers, but they were not basketball skills. So I waited and practiced and waited some more. But then one day I was chosen. Not because of my skills or desire to play, in truth not because of my efforts to improve, but I was picked because I was there trying to get picked. Jesus has picked some of us to be on His team as well. Not because we act so good or because we are the first one to church, or because we know all of the popular phrases and we got our church step perfected. God has picked us because God has had mercy on us. We have humbled ourselves. We are living in a manner that tells God that we are trying to be picked for the team. Beloved, we can clamor and shout all we want, but in the end God will make the Call to decide who will be on the team and who will not.

My Prayer for Today:

The Lord's Lesson on Prayer

"One of his disciples said to him, 'Lord teach us how to pray, as John taught his disciples.' "
LUKE 11:1

Today's Prayer

Loving God, show me, teach me how to pray in a manner that is meaningful and not trite. I don't always pray in earnest, sometimes I am just going through the motions; sometimes I am too angry with others or myself to pray. But show me, teach me how to pray in a manner that is meaningful and pleasing to you. Amen.

Today's Reflection

There are lots of formulas that people use to organize prayer. We have liturgies and prayer cloths, we have postures and special words, but do we have God's attention? At the core of Jesus' prayer response to being asked about how to pray is the need to honor God. We honor God not by heaping up a string of special names for God. We honor God not by having fancy introductions to our prayers or by having carefully worded sentences. We honor God not by going all over the place waiting for somebody in the congregation to react to what we say. We honor God by how sincere we are when we pray for God's Will to be done in our lives. We honor God by being merciful to others, as God has shown us mercy. That is what Jesus was teaching the disciples when he taught them how to pray.

My Prayer for Today:

When God Pays Back Evil

"Woe to the guilty! How unfortunate they are, for what their hands have done shall be done to them."

ISAIAH 3:11

Today's Prayer

All-powerful God, look upon me with mercy today. Lord, forgive me for my sins and let me live this day with a clean heart. Gracious God, I bow before your throne in humble submission to your authority in my life and over the entire world. Amen.

Today's Reflection

In this chapter of Isaiah, God is mad and is about to address the wrongs against the people in court. God's argument and judgment are one and the same and some heads are about to roll. God is not pleased with the way those in charge are treating the poor. God is not happy the way some flaunt what God has provided over those who have not benefited from God's bounty. Some people like to play God as if God does not exist or does not care about what goes on in the world. God will hold us all accountable for how we treat those who are poor and in need. Who, in your life, did God place that made a positive difference for you? Okay, in whose life will you return the favor?

My Prayer for Today:

Corrected Vision

"Blessed are the pure in heart, for they will see God."
MATTHEW 5:8

Today's Prayer

Most Holy God, I awake this day and thank you for the splendor of life. I am thankful for last night's rest and for a safe place to have laid my head. Let me have a joyful and loving heart so that in love I may see your face today. Amen.

Today's Reflection

What does pure mean? Does it mean 100% of an essence or mineral? Perhaps, but let's say it means something that has been purified, something that has been tested as if it has been through a refiner's fire. Jesus, in this famous passage, says that the pure in heart will see God. Those who have been tested, are those like Job who, when others told him to curse God and die, refused. Our world is constantly pulling us to have a compromised heart, some good and some not so good. Go ahead, says the whisper in your head, "God knows your heart." Sure, God does and knows that it is not pure. Right now, open your heart to God and ask God to come in and refine it for you, to make it pure. So you can see God in your life and how God is working for you.

My Prayer for Today:

Day 27

Half-full Faith

"Where you go, I will go; where you lodge, I will lodge;
your people shall be my people, and your God my God."
RUTH 1:16b

Today's Prayer

Holy God, we pray for faith to see rainbows after floods, new life after death, and gifts from you in the midst of our losses. In Jesus' name. Amen.

Today's Reflection

In one of my favorite novels, a little boy is kidnapped while in the care of his big brother. Paralyzed by grief, their mother cannot appreciate what she has left—a son and daughter who need her, and a husband who loves her. Like this fictional mother, Naomi lost so much while in Moab: her husband and two sons were dead. Naomi was unable to appreciate what she had left.

Like Naomi, we may feel bitter, that life has dealt harsh or unfair blows. Let us pray for faith to claim the gifts that come to us even in the midst of our tragedies and losses.

My Prayer for Today:

Well-Watered Trees

*"They are like trees planted by streams of water, which
yield their fruit in its season, and their leaves do not
wither."*

PSALM 1:3

Today's Prayer

Lord God, refresh us with the living water, that our faith may be
strong. Keep us deeply rooted in your Word and in your love. In
Jesus' name. Amen.

Today's Reflection

When my parents bought their home in Chicago, it was quite a
momentous occasion. The house represented for them security and a
place to grow things—children, gardens, and plants. What they
touch is full of life. The plants grew strong, tall, and sturdy, like well-
watered trees.

Mom and Dad are like well-watered trees—strong and sturdy in
their faith and their faithfulness to their family. They, like many of
our ancestors who have gone before them, delight in God's law. They
read it and pray over it. May we, who come from a strong people,
know the love of God expressed in God's commands to us. May we
be like trees planted by streams of water.

My Prayer for Today:

Day 29

Don't Yield to Temptations

*"Jesus, full of the Holy Spirit, returned from the Jordan and
was led by the Spirit into the wilderness."*

LUKE 4:1

Today's Prayer

Holy God, help me as I seek to overcome the temptations that
come at me from every side. I am tempted to eat too much, smoke
too much, talk too much, and even sneak around too much. God
help me to fight against those things that feel good, but are not always good for me. Amen.

Today's Reflection

Because God loves justice, take confidence that God will allow
you to speak against the injustices that you experience or see in this
world. God has not abandoned the world. God is still our refuge in
the time of trouble, especially for those who dare to confront evil.
Living a transformed life means living in the knowledge that sticking
one's neck out can lead to serious consequences, but consider a turtle which can never get anywhere on its own unless it sticks its neck
out. If God will protect a turtle, then know that God will also protect
you.

My Prayer for Today:

Don't Build Traps for Others

*"So they hanged Haman on the gallows that he had
prepared for Mordecai. Then the anger of the king abated."*
ESTHER 7:10

Today's Prayer

God, I live in a cynical world where it seems those who plot and
scheme ill will against others are the ones who get ahead. Sometimes,
Lord, it feels like I should just let it all hang out, go for broke, do
whatever it takes to get ahead. So what if I cheat a little today, God? I
will make it up to you. Lord, help me to do what is right so I won't
get caught in a trap of my own design. Amen.

Today's Reflection

How gruesome being hanged, especially on the gallows that one
built to hang someone else? Do you know somebody who is trying to
build gallows for you? Take heart from this story that there is hope,
that when others seek to do you in that they themselves will fall vic-
tim of their own evil schemes. I have seen it happen time and time
again, people falling into the very traps they tried to set for someone
else. The Gospels are full of stories where the religious leaders tried
to set traps for Jesus, only to find themselves caught. So beloved, if
you must build something, build bridges of love and reconciliation.
That is what God wants.

My Prayer for Today:

Day 31

A New Appointment

"So Esther set Mordecai over the house of Haman."
ESTHER 8:2

Today's Prayer

Loving God, life can be such a challenge, help me to make the right decisions and walk in the path that you have set for me. Amen.

Today's Reflection

Are you prepared to handle an unexpected promotion? How about a new job that puts you in charge of others. How will you handle the responsibility? Mordecai was given a new job and he used his new position to help his people, not just to help himself. Mordecai was now a truly favored person and he used his new appointment to keep his people from dying. But Mordecai could not do it by himself; he had help from Esther. Esther and Mordecai as a team, with Esther taking the lead, turned the tables on someone who had evil in his heart. And when they were rewarded, they used their power for the benefit of others. May we do likewise.

My Prayer for Today:

Honoring God

*"Or do you not know that your body is a temple of the
Holy Spirit within you, which you have from God, and that
you are not your own?"*

1 CORINTHIANS 6:19

Today's Prayer

Thank you God for creating me. Lord, I will live this day being re-minded that my body is a dwelling place for your Holy Spirit. I will refrain from doing things that go against your will. I will listen to your voice as you guide me through life. Amen.

Today's Reflection

Think of it: inside of you is the Holy creative force that called the world into existence. God's Holy Spirit is inside of you, speaking to you, giving you sound advice. Alas, too many of us don't want to lis-ten to God; instead we listen to the clanging sounds of a highly com-petitive society. We listen to the groan of our loins and play the songs of immorality and easy pleasures. Listen; again incline your ear to that voice of righteousness that wants only the best for you. Yes, some-times it seems doing what is right is hard but in the end the reward for obedience is great. Honor God, not just with your lips or with a handclap, but honor God with your entire being, refrain from evil, bypass immorality, and show love to others.

My Prayer for Today:

Getting a Hearing

*"We know that God does not listen to sinners, but he does
listen to one who worships and obeys his will."*

JOHN 9:31

Today's Prayer

Gracious God, help me to live my life in a manner that when I
pray you will give me a hearing. God, help me to treat people that I
encounter not as the world would treat them but as you desire. God,
let me live from the inside out under the guidance of the Holy Spirit
so all that I do is pleasing to you. Amen.

Today's Reflection

The justification for a man being able to see was argued that it was
based on one's ability to be heard. The religious leaders questioned
this man who was born blind. How did you receive your sight? The
former blind man indicated that it was Jesus who healed him. In the
minds of the Pharisees, Jesus could not be of God because he healed
this man on the Sabbath, and they continued to question the man.
After another round of questioning the former blind man stated, "I
don't know the man but what I do know is that I was blind but now
I can see." God heard his prayer and responded. Beloved, what evidence do you need to know that Jesus is real and cares for you? Do
you want to get a hearing from God? Then do God's will and walk in
the way of the Lord.

My Prayer for Today:

Day 34

Boat Rides

*"And early in the morning he came walking toward them
on the sea."*
MATTHEW 14:25

Today's Prayer

Loving God, help me learn to relax and to have more trust in you.
I try hard to put all my trust in you; help me to do a better job than
I have in the past. Today I will trust and believe that you want the
very best for me and I will act accordingly. Amen.

Today's Reflection

If chapter 14 is the events of one day, then Jesus had a very full
day. It is a day that starts with the murder of his cousin, him trying to
grieve, having to heal people, then feed them, preaching is somewhere in the mix, and all of this concludes by evening which found
him in prayer. And much of what happened, Jesus had to do for
himself. Have you ever lost a loved one, but the demands of the day
did not permit you time to yourself to grieve? Were you the one who
had to be strong for the rest of the family? Well, Jesus knows what
you went through, and while others were resting and visiting, Jesus
was taking care of business. Have faith, Jesus is with you. Have faith,
knowing that Jesus will walk on water if necessary to come get into
the boat of your situation. Okay, look around; do you sense that
Jesus is with you? Now the storms will not seem so bad. Go handle
your business knowing that Jesus is with you.

My Prayer for Today:

Nice Car But No Gas

"Desire without knowledge is not good, and one who moves too hurriedly misses the way."

PROVERBS 19:2

Today's Prayer

Oh Lord, sometimes I feel like an empty vessel. God, I am fine on the outside; all of my appearance is top shelf. I know that I am a prize, but I feel empty sometimes, not quite full. Lord, fill the void in my life that causes me to go in the wrong direction. Amen.

Today's Reflection

A friend of mine, back in the day, always drove big expensive cars around on one or two dollars' worth of gas. He had these beautiful automotive machines but could not go very far. We have a lot of people today becoming ministers, getting television shows; some even have nice-sized congregations. Some, not all, of these ministers are self-proclaimed; they have a lot of energy but they don't have any real life experience, and all they can offer people are slogans. They have the zeal but they lack knowledge; they are hasty to make a name for themselves so they can walk around with their chest stuck out. But they don't know the way and will soon find themselves stumbling in the forest of cheap, feel good but can't sustain you theology. Their zeal and haste have made a mess. Friends, slow down, remember all that feels good is not necessarily good for you. It's like being stuck in the middle of nowhere in a nice car but with no gas.

My Prayer for Today:

Staying Put

*"The Lord appeared to Isaac and said, 'Do not go
down to Egypt, settle in the land that I shall
show you.' "*

GENESIS 26:2

Today's Prayer

Oh Gracious God, help my restless soul to be still. I am so ready to make a move to do something else with my life, I don't know what and I almost don't care, I just want to move on. But God, please still me so I will make the best decision possible and not make one out of boredom or foolishness, or worse, trying to fulfill the dreams or expectations of others. Loving God, speak to me and provide for me a clear path to follow and a perfect place to lay my head. Thank you. Amen.

Today's Reflection

Isaac was ready to go, times were hard, there was a famine in the land and Isaac was ready to jump on the next thing going to Egypt. But God said stay put in Gerar. Do you feel like you are in a Gerar? Do you work for a company that doesn't seem to appreciate you or your skills? Do you have any skills that the company can use? If not then get some, if yes then use them to benefit the organization that you are working for. In other words, build your wells where you are; even if someone else comes along and tries to claim credit for your work, respond by building another well. It will not always be easy, but dig deep, build wells until you are the best in the company at doing what you do. Become invaluable, and when it is time for you to move God will make it plain with an offer you will not be able to refuse.

My Prayer for Today:

Day 37

Do What I Tell You

"God also spoke to Moses and said to him: 'I am the Lord.' "
EXODUS 6:2

Today's Prayer

God, I know that I resist you from time to time. I know that I act like I can do things my way and not show any concern for what you want. Loving God, I have made many senseless mistakes in my life; help me to change and realize that you are Lord. Amen.

Today's Reflection

Moses got on God's nerves with all of his whining and reluctance. I know something about this. Here God had to remind Moses who was Lord and say, go do what I tell you to do. There is no more debate, no more discussion, just go, get a move on, people are waiting to be freed. Is God saying the same thing to you? What has God told you to do that you are still resisting? Trust God that what God has called you to do, you will be prepared for it. In fact you may already be up for the task, you just need to be encouraged. Know that God is the Lord.

My Prayer for Today:

Be Not Deceived

"And he said, Beware that you are not led astray;
for many will come in my name claiming 'I am
he!' and, 'The time is near!' Do not go
after them."

LUKE 21:8

Today's Prayer

Jesus, there are so many competing messages these days for my time and money. Buy this, go there, come here, and buy this thing as well. All these messages are telling me that I am nothing without them. But not just advertisers, churches are all claiming that they know what you want for me. Help me, Jesus, to know which way to go. Amen.

Today's Reflection

Jesus warns his disciples that fantastic facades will often have fatal finishes. Just because it looks good does not mean God has ordained it for you. No matter how many people are going there and no matter how many fancy cars are in the lot, it does not mean it is the place for you. Now, big churches are okay: 3,000 joined the church in one day on the day of Pentecost. Instead, listen closely to the message. Is it a message from God or is it a message that you are uttering to God that is being repeated from the lips of this minister? Is it a message for your ears or is it a message for your heart? God knows your desires; most people want financial security and even wealth, so to hear some preacher telling you that God wants you to prosper is not news, nor is it a message that speaks to your heart. Be firm in the Lord and you will gain all that God has planned for your life.

My Prayer for Today:

No Justice, No Peace

"The Lord rises to argue his case; he stands to judge the peoples."
ISAIAH 3:13

Today's Prayer

Thank you for our leaders, Father. Their jobs loom large over the daily struggles for justice and peace. Guide the footsteps of those of us who lead and those who follow that we may do so wisely. Amen.

Today's Reflection

Justice issues still loom large in our communities. While issues such as unfairness in the criminal justice system and unfair business practices are only a few of the issues our brothers and sisters deal with on a daily basis, our hope lies in Jesus. Statistics may show us what we're up against, but the numbers cannot measure up to God's justice. Moreover, we can be assured that God is ever present in our daily struggles. God will have the final say.

As we start each day, acknowledge the men and women in your life and others who make a difference. Thank God for those who lead, teach, and protect. God will strengthen us spiritually and mentally so that we can do our jobs. If we remember to do what God asks of us in our capacity as leaders and as followers, God will take care of the rest.

My Prayer for Today:

Hope Will Not Disappoint

"But the one who endures to the end will be saved."
MATTHEW 24:13

Today's Prayer

Father, give me hope. When I see the pain and sorrow of others, help me to hold on. Help me to be ready. Lord, keep me faithful and help me endure to the end. Amen.

Today's Reflection

The little girl sat in the pew next to her grandmother. She listened intently to the words of the minister. Later, at dinner while her parents, aunts, and uncles laughed, it seemed, without a care in the world, the girl questioned her grandmother. How could they be so carefree? Wasn't the end near? After all, that was what she heard.

Like the forecasts of the stock exchange, many predictions are presented as the truth. Over and over again, forecasts fall short of the reality. Like the little girl, we must ask the question, but not out of fear. God calls us to be faithful. God wants us to believe in him. Here is what the grandmother said to the little girl: "We don't know the time or place, child, but Jesus is coming back. We know only that we must love God and love each other and do what is right. If you do that, my little one, God will always be there for you."

My Prayer for Today:

Day 41

The Blessing of Life

*"But thanks be to God, who in Christ always leads us in
triumphal procession, and through us spreads in every
place the fragrance that comes from knowing him."*
2 CORINTHIANS 2:14

Today's Prayer

Knowing you, Lord, has been the blessing of life. Without you,
my life would have no meaning. Reaffirm your love for me as only
you can. Place your holy smell upon me so that others may come to
know of you. Amen.

Today's Reflection

The young white male asked the beautiful black woman why she
proclaimed God. It didn't make sense that she could possibly love a
God that allowed her ancestors to be slaves. The black woman smiled.
She told the young man, "You don't know like I know." Perhaps the
question belies the need for the young man to be convinced of the
power of God. If this black woman could love God, perhaps he, too,
could. Looking at the bigger picture, the question begs for clarity on
the part of the believer. It doesn't mean using fancy words or witty
clichés. It means straight talk. When Paul came to the true understanding of the Christ, he wanted to do more than proclaim it. He
didn't want people to follow God out of a misguided notion associated with other religions. He wanted people to be drawn to and led
by God through God's own fragrance of life. Give God a chance and
you, too, will see.

My Prayer for Today:

Day 42

A Closer Walk

"If any of you is lacking in wisdom, ask God, who gives to all generously and ungrudgingly, and it will be given to you."
JAMES 1:5

Today's Prayer

Speak through me every day, Lord. Let your words speak volumes to those in need. Give me wisdom to follow you faithfully and to use this wisdom to proclaim your word. Amen.

Today's Reflection

Getting stronger in your walk with Christ is God's plan in action. As your faith strengthens, your hope for humankind increases. God's generosity is shown when we knowingly ask of God, believing that our unselfish wants will be granted.

Over time, tests will come. Our struggle comes when our needs and wants are out of step with what God wants from us. In the book of James, we are given the tools to stay in step with God. First, we must ask. It is not that God doesn't know what we need. Sometimes we must ask of God what God would have us ask. That's all right! James shows us the source for it all. When we realize where the source is, we become lights upon the path. As we lean on him, we can manifest the attributes of those who love God. As James points out, leaning on God rids us of destructive behaviors and puts us in step with God's will for our lives. So ask. God is waiting.

My Prayer for Today:

Day 43

Get Up and Go

"Now the Lord said to Abram, 'Go from your country and your kindred and your father's house to the land that I will show you.' So Abram went as the Lord had told him."
GENESIS 12:1

Today's Prayer

Lord, give me the peace that comes from knowledge of your love and protection. Let your holy wind stir me from apathy and light a fire that can be seen in all that I do and say. Amen.

Today's Reflection

What faith! The Lord says, "Go," and according to the account that has been handed down to us, Abram seems to take off without question or hesitation. God does not even tell Abram where he is going, only that he should leave behind everything that is familiar and familial and go to "the land that I will show you." What faith! It was an amazing thing then as now, in the 21st century, with all our long-range planning and strategies. It takes great faith to take off without a full understanding of what lies ahead. The first step is to get up and go, and do whatever we are called to do for the sake of the gospel—knowing that whatever happens, we go with God.

My Prayer for Today:

The Stand

"If you keep silent at such a time as this . . . you will perish."
ESTHER 4:14

Today's Prayer

Lord God, throughout history your prophets have struggled to proclaim your Will and your Word. We, too, are called to share our resources and care for all your creation. Loosen our tongues to speak out against evil in all its forms. Amen.

Today's Reflection

"Why was I ever born?" The lament of many a teenager, in every generation, and probably even you. These words are usually uttered when some well-meaning plan has fallen through. But questioning the why and wherefore of the circumstances of one's birth is a serious theological step. Why are you where you are right now?

All blessings come from God, but they come through human agents. People sit in churches every week and pray for those who are homeless, and those who are sick, and those who suffer from injustices. But who will be moved to speak out against those injustices? What is the face of the homeless person and what are we doing to make sure that God's will is done? God does not will that people sleep in doorways, or that children go hungry. It may be easier to retreat to our comfort zones, but the problem is that the comfort zone is always shrinking. And sooner or later we will be moved to take a stand—one way or the other. If we do not speak out against evil, then through our silence we speak up for evil.

My Prayer for Today:

Day 45

Real Love

"Love never ends."
1 CORINTHIANS 13:8

Today's Prayer

Lord, teach us how to love each other, how to forgive one another, how to bear each other's burdens, how to share each other's joys, and even how to laugh with each other. We pray that you would bind us with cords that cannot be broken, so that in community we may continually feel your loving presence among us. Amen.

Today's Reflection

It has been said of 1 Corinthians 13 that if you substitute the word Christ for the word love, you will have a better understanding of what Paul was trying to say to the people in the church at Corinth. This kind of love is no ordinary, human love. It is the love of the one who gave up equality with God to live among us, who died because of us, but who conquered death for us and loves us still. This kind of love is a model for everyone in Christ to achieve.

My Prayer for Today:

Day 46

The Idleness of Idleness

"Go to the ant, O sluggard; consider her ways, and be wise."

PROVERBS 6:6

Today's Prayer

Lord, take me and use me for the building of your kingdom. Wake up your church, lest we die in our sleep. Make us ever vigilant for your Word and your Will. Make in us that apathy for the gospel, and idleness, may not be our sins. Amen.

Today's Reflection

Have you ever seen an ant at rest? That is not to say that ants don't rest, just that they always seem to be working. Is this the wisdom that is being imparted? As people of God, we are commanded to sanctify the holy day, take a day of re-creation, even rest. But let us be reminded that it is one day of rest per week and not seven. We have all received some God-given talent. It is our sacred obligation to return to God what has been given, whether it be artistic abilities or business and organization skills. Some people put a lot of effort into exercising on a regular basis. But what are we doing for the kingdom of God? Are we working just one hour a week? Go to the ant, O sluggard. Consider her ways and be wise.

My Prayer for Today:

Staying Salty

"You are the salt of the earth, but if salt has lost its taste,
how shall its saltiness be restored? It is no longer good for
anything."
MATTHEW 5:13

Today's Prayer

O Lord, my God, I pray that you keep me near you. Keep my faith in you strong, and actions toward others loving, so that I may able to serve you through the best and worst of what happens in my life. Amen.

Today's Reflection

With all the warnings about cutting back on salt in our diets, we might think this is no longer a good metaphor—but think again. We will always have salt with us. It literally is in our blood. Christians are an integral part of the cosmos—and just like salt, some are better for the cosmos than others. The question we must each ask of ourselves is this:

"Am I the good stuff or the not-so-good stuff?" In Baptism we were made new creations in Christ, who fought the battle of sin and won.

But in response to the work of Christ, we are called to be more than just seasoning. In Jesus' time, salting food meant the difference between being able to have something to eat or going hungry because the food was not preserved. Today, our participation in the life of the church can mean the difference between someone being spiritually fed or going hungry—and that someone may be you.

My Prayer for Today:

The Transformers

*"Do not be conformed to this world, but be transformed by
the renewal of your mind."*

ROMANS 12:2

Today's Prayer

Awesome God, source of life, healing, and strength, you alone
hold our times in your hands, and you alone know the ending to the
story of our lives. Calm the raging storms that plague my life, and let
me surrender fully to your will. Let me feel the joy of your salvation,
and let that joy glorify you, that others may know the healing power
of your love in Jesus Christ. Amen.

Today's Reflection

Several years ago, there was a popular line of robot-like toys on
the market called "Transformers." The concept was that with some
slight adjustments—a turn of an arm, a twist of a leg, a pushing
down on the head—the robot would "transform" into an entirely different toy, such as a car or plane. The toys were a hit because the
transformation took place in just moments. Anyone who is in Christ
knows that real transformation takes a lifetime to accomplish. It is
not simply a mere adjustment here and there that turns us into
changed beings. It starts with water and the Word in Holy Baptism.
Then, we spend the rest of our lives fulfilling our baptismal promises
of study, prayer, praise, thanksgiving, and being a worker of the
kingdom of God. Through the repetitive actions of being a member
of the body of Christ, transformation takes place.

My Prayer for Today:

Day 49

Requiem

"If the foundations are destroyed, what can the righteous do?"
PSALM 11:3

Today's Prayer

Lord God, comfort with the grace of your Holy Spirit all who are surrounded by the shadow of death. Give them courage, peace, and joy—the joy that only those who live and die in you can know. Comfort those who mourn with the hope of eternal life with those they love. Amen.

Today's Reflection

In an adult Sunday morning class, one woman recounted her story of surviving a tornado: "As I saw the spinning dust cloud in the distance, I was seized with fear. I knew that was the day I would die, and I prayed to God to let it be a quick death. No cuts or lacerations, no concussions or brain damage, just quick and painless."

"You lost your faith in God!" shouted one participant in the group.

"People die every day. Isn't that what funerals are all about?" the woman countered. It was an eye-opener for many others that day.

We all consider it a blessing to escape a close call, but what about when one does not escape? What do we call that? The psalmist tells us there is no place to run except to the Lord—especially when we seem to face a sure and certain death. We believe that the grave is only a gate, because we are in Christ. Whether we live or die, we are in Christ.

My Prayer for Today:

Trusting in the Promises of God

"Abram believed the Lord; and the Lord reckoned it to him as righteousness."

GENESIS 15:6, NIV

Today's Prayer

To the God whose promises are true and overflowing, let me never doubt that what you have said will come true. I depend on your promises daily, for they are what carry me through. Help me to believe in you with the same fervency as Abraham. Amen.

Today's Reflection

The time for Abraham's death was drawing near. Abraham was becoming concerned that he had no heir in whom to leave his estate. God told Abraham not to worry, for he would have a son. Abraham came to believe in the provision and the faithfulness of God.

We, too, can develop a right relationship with God. God has a plan for our lives. It is up to us to cultivate our relationship with God to hear that plan. God's promises are true, for God will protect and provide everything that we need.

My Prayer for Today:

Taking Courage

*"On the third day Esther put on her royal robes and stood
in the inner court of the king's palace, opposite the king's
hall. The king was sitting on his royal throne inside the
palace opposite the entrance to the palace."*

ESTHER 5:1–3

Today's Prayer

I thank you, God, for the courage to face my challenges daily.
Teach me not to be afraid of what the consequence could be when I
take a stand. May your love strengthen me as I leave my comfort
zone and risk to do things differently. Amen.

Today's Reflection

God wants us to face our challenges with courage. God wants us
to look them in the eye and take a stand. Esther knew she was risking her life to go before the king without being summoned. But she
was determined to help her people; she knew that the destruction of
the Jews was at stake and she had to do something. Like Esther,
when faced with difficult decisions, we too should not fear or doubt
that God is able to help us meet our challenges. We are to stand firm,
take courage, go before our God in prayer. Just as God saved the
Jews through the courage of Esther, God will save us, if we have
courage and faith.

My Prayer for Today:

Wait with Patience

"How long must I wrestle with my thoughts and every day have sorrow in my heart? How long will my enemy triumph over me?"

PSALM 13:2, NIV

Today's Prayer

To my Savior Jesus Christ, I thank you for your presence in my life when I need you most. Lord, I know that you hear my cry and will answer when the time is right. I will wait and wait on you, Lord, until you have decided what is best for me. Amen.

Today's Reflection

Waiting on the Lord is not always easy. We tend to be anxious and uptight, and to put too much nervous thought into our situation. Our thoughts get cloudy and we cannot always remember what God did for us the last time we were in a difficult place. In our cloudiness, if we can remember how God has brought us through many a storm, then it would be easier to wait on God. Putting the focus on God and not the problem makes the waiting easier. When we wait patiently on God, no matter how the situation looks, God will work things out for our good pleasure.

My Prayer for Today:

Day 53

Know Where You Are Going

*"All at once he followed her like an ox going to the
slaughter . . ."*
PROVERBS 7:22, NIV

Today's Prayer

Oh God, I pray for your wisdom for my life that comes from knowing your word. May the word give guidance to my life and assist me to walk in your path. Lord, speak now that I might follow your will for my life. Amen.

Today's Reflection

In our text, because this man did not understand God's vision for his life, he was walking down the wrong road and encountered an immoral woman. Because he did not have God's vision for his life, he could not resist the sweet and seductive works of the temptress. People who don't know God's vision for their lives spend their time wandering aimlessly down the wrong roads. A lack of direction and inquiry for guidance allows them to be vulnerable to many and diverse temptations. Knowing God's Word gives us wisdom to avoid the pitfalls that lead us down the road to temptation. Knowing God's Word helps us to discern God's direction for our lives. Read and study for God's direction in your life that you may be put on the right road to a fulfilled future.

My Prayer for Today:

Day 54

Does God Know You?

"Not everyone who says to me, 'Lord, Lord,' will enter the kingdom of heaven, but only he who does the will of my Father who is heaven."

MATTHEW 7:21, NIV

Today's Prayer

God, give me true mercy and compassion for hurting and needy people. May I show my love for you by visiting the sick, clothing the naked, feeding the hungry, and being with those in prison. Amen.

Today's Reflection

There are many people who perform the correct ritual and the right religious observance, but for the wrong reasons and wrong motivation of heart. The right religious observance is not enough. We must be able to truly live the word in our own lives, showing our obedience to the Savior that we might receive our reward in heaven.

God says in this text that everyone who does right religious observance will not enter the kingdom of God. Everyone who quotes the word of God is not necessarily in right relationship with God. The text says, "Not everyone who says to me, 'Lord, Lord,' will enter the kingdom of God." The Christian that acts out his biblical faith among the poor and needy is the one who can say, "Lord, Lord," and enter the kingdom.

My Prayer for Today:

God Accepts the Weak to Make Them Strong

"Welcome those who are weak in faith, but not for the purpose of quarreling over opinions."

ROMANS 14:1

Today's Prayer

Loving God, the one who is accepting of everyone, I thank you for how understanding you are of me when I don't always have the right answers. I know that sometimes my thinking is off the mark, but thank you for sticking with me and urging me to turn my thinking around. It is because of the love you show me that I can show that same love to others. Amen.

Today's Reflection

In the church there are different levels of Christian maturity. Each person has decided what to believe in his heart and usually there are many very different perceptions of right and wrong. Many people answer the very same question differently. Paul is saying to us in this verse that those of us who are seasoned in our faith are not to criticize those who have not experienced Christ in the way we have. Paul advises us to give people time to mature and discover God's truth in their own lives. Most of us can remember times when we adamantly believed or practiced something, and time and experience came to show us that our thinking and behavior needed adjustment. God was patient with us as we were growing. Paul admonishes us to have the same patience with others that God had for us.

My Prayer for Today:

Maintain the Unity of the Spirit

*"May God who gives endurance and encouragement give
you a spirit of unity among yourselves as you follow Christ
Jesus."*

ROMANS 15:5, NIV

Today's Prayer

Gracious God, peace is what we desire today. There is conflict
everywhere. May we strive together to maintain the unity of the spirit
in the church. May we truly become one, that we would show love
and forgiveness one to another. May we rely on your Spirit that gives
endurance, encouragement, and unity. Amen.

Today's Reflection

This text points out that we cannot get unity out of our own efforts. We must realize that God gives unity to the church. We must
strive to maintain the unity of the Spirit by living in faith and giving
situations of conflict and unforgiveness to God, acknowledging that
God is able to work things out in God's own time and God's own
way. Our task is to keep our eyes on God and not each other. If we
keep our eyes on God and the unity of the Spirit, we will not be self-
centered, but concerned for others. Our daily attitude will reflect the
endurance and encouragement that will unite the people of God together in Christian love.

My Prayer for Today:

Day 57

Anxiety

"You are the God who sees me . . ."
GENESIS 16:13

Today's Prayer

Heavenly Father, may we always seek your guidance and wisdom for all of our decisions. May we always walk in your will and in your ways. Amen.

Today's Reflection

It's hard to imagine a wife asking another woman to conceive her husband's child. Yet this is what Sarah asked Hagar. She wanted to make sure that Abraham had an heir. Sarah didn't think of God's power, nor the question: "Is there anything too hard for the Lord?" (Genesis 18:14). She wanted results. Hagar obeyed and conceived, but animosity set in between the two women. Hagar fled to the desert to escape Sarah's anger. In her brokenness and desperation, God came to her with a word of comfort and hope. Hagar said, "You are the God who sees me." In our despair, we can be assured that God will also see us.

My Prayer for Today:

Day 58

Empowered to Trust in God

"The midwives however feared God."
EXODUS 1:17

Today's Prayer

Kind and loving Father, bless us with the understanding that we are made strong by adversity. Teach us to accept your will for our lives, whether it's in joy, sadness, or trials. Amen.

Today's Reflection

The Hebrew midwives Shiprah and Puah were given a cruel command by Pharaoh: "Kill the male babies that are born." Those words by the king put extreme pressure on those women, life if they obeyed the king and death if they didn't.

Pressures and adversities in life are built-in facets of living. They are inevitable. They will come our way sooner or later. God empowered them to disobey the order of the king. They were rewarded for their faithfulness. The same Holy Spirit that empowered the Hebrew midwives will do the same for you.

My Prayer for Today:

Our God Will Satisfy

"My soul will be satisfied as with the richest of foods; with singing lips my mouth will praise you."

PSALM 63:5, NIV

Today's Prayer

Praise the Lord! Praise the Lord! Lord, we are satisfied in you. You have done so many great things in our lives and we are satisfied with you. Words cannot express how grateful we are that you are in our lives. And for our satisfaction we glorify and adore thee, giving thee honor and praise. Amen.

Today's Reflection

When David was in the wilderness hiding from his enemies, he felt discouraged, uncertain, and alone. David called on the Lord. In this place of wilderness and starvation, David praised God and proclaimed that God would satisfy him, and did.

There are times when we, too, are in difficult places, when emotional stress and tension are high. In those times, we are to look to God. We are to open our mouths and to praise God, proclaim the blessings of God, and bring forth praises to God. Just as God met David in the wilderness, God will comfort us.

My Prayer for Today:

A Dwelling Place in God

"Lord, who may dwell in your sanctuary?"
PSALM 15:1

Today's Prayer

O Gracious God, may the rays of your glory illumine our hearts. May we dwell in your presence in humility and gratitude. Amen.

Today's Reflection

"Lord, who may dwell in your sanctuary?" is a valid question. It's not who may visit, but who may dwell and "Who may live on your holy hill?" Each of us is confronted by the same question. How do we answer? The psalmist gave the criterion for the dwelling place in God. It is a place of quiet rest and peace. It is here that we can bring all of our cares and concerns to God. We have security to keep us safe in the midst of Satan's attacks. We find shelter and rest in the shadow of the Most High. It is in our relationship with God that we have the assurance of dwelling in his presence, his sanctuary, and his holy hill.

My Prayer for Today:

Day 61

Faith in Action

"Go! It will be done just as you believed it would . . ."
MATTHEW 8:13

Today's Prayer

Compassionate God, look on us with compassion. Increase our faith and grant us the ability to know how to trust and act on your word. Amen.

Today's Reflection

"Go! It will be done just as you believed it would." The humility of the centurion reminds us that we must come to Jesus in faith. Our lives are governed by faith—however, doubt can negate faith. As a man of limited power, the centurion had grasped the fact that he had encountered the One with limitless power. Out of his humility he made his request: "Lord, I do not deserve to have you come under my roof, but just say the word, and my servant will be healed." Jesus hears and answers our prayers. He is not bound by time, space, or circumstances. Our responsibility is to trust him and act on his word. Faith is not only believing, but action as well.

My Prayer for Today:

Day 62

Temptations Will Come

"When the Devil had finished all this tempting, he left him until an opportune time."

LUKE 4:13

Today's Prayer

Gracious Father, empower me through the Holy Spirit to withstand the temptations and not yield to them. Amen.

Today's Reflection

Jesus has shown us how to overcome temptations. They will come! Usually in our moments of vulnerability, we encounter the enemy of our soul. His ways are subtle and sneaky. Satan chooses every opportunity available to tempt us away from God. He awaits his moments in order to be effective.

There are all kinds of temptations that will come into our lives. We can be strengthened or we can succumb to them. We have the scriptures to empower us. Jesus didn't argue with this enemy; he simply said, "It is written. . . ." We can do the same.

My Prayer for Today:

Day 63

Unity in Christ

"That all of you agree with one another . . ."
1 CORINTHIANS 10

Today's Prayer

Loving Father, disagreements will come. May we be able to disagree and do it lovingly, not in hatred or strife. May we always remember that we are a royal priesthood and a holy nation. Amen.

Today's Reflection

Strife within the Body of Christ is divisive and destructive. We are called to be one, united by God's gift of salvation to all. We are not called to be clones of another, nor agree with everything. It is the abiding presence of the Holy Spirit that will prevent our disagreements from becoming acrimonious. Christ binds and empowers us to fulfill the command that we have been given.

My Prayer for Today:

Day 64

All Things Are Possible

"Is anything too wonderful for the Lord?"
GENESIS 18:14

Today's Prayer

Dear God, please help me in my doubt so that I can face life's obstacles with the knowledge that all things are possible with you. Amen.

Today's Reflection

Is anything too wonderful for the Lord? "At the set time I will return to you, in due season, and Sarah shall have a son." Life is filled with challenges, obstacles, and tunnels that seem to have no light at the end. Yet, when we read Genesis 18:14, we can be assured that God is with us and that there is nothing too hard for the Lord. In verse 14 the Lord is removing an obstacle that seems impossible to remove by assuring Abraham and Sarah that Sarah will conceive and have a son. What the Lord is saying here to Abraham and Sarah, the Lord is also saying to us—that all things are possible with God.

My Prayer for Today:

Egoism Is a Sin of Pride

"Who is there the king would rather honor than me?"
ESTHER 6:7

Today's Prayer

Merciful God, forgive our selfish pride and egotistical behavior. Teach us to love one another in our diversity as you love us. Amen.

Today's Reflection

Selfishness, hidden anger, and resentment of others will ultimately manifest itself in hatred. Haman despised Mordecai; his hatred became like smoldering embers of fire awaiting the right time to flare up. Haman methodically devised ways that would ensure the destruction of his Jewish adversary, even if it meant killing all Jews. Ironically, he designed the method of death for himself; for Haman was hung on the gallows he built for Mordecai.

Racial, gender, and cultural bigotry are insidious. The tentacles of bigotry become suction cups of hatred, disabling all humanity. But the joys of diversity within humanity reflect the beauty of God.

My Prayer for Today:

Anger, Rage, and Violence

"The king rose from the feast in wrath and went into the palace garden, but Haman stayed to beg his life from Queen Esther, for he saw that the king was determined to destroy him."

ESTHER 7:7

Today's Prayer

Lord, let your peace rule in my heart that I might be able to control my anger and rage. Amen.

Today's Reflection

The king rose from the feast in wrath. Sudden and uncontrolled anger was common for King Ahasuerus. How common is it in our lives? Our lives are so stressful that often we live only one word or comment away from the same kind of anger and rage displayed by the king. We see, on an increasing scale, the rise in violence resulting from anger and rage. Road rage is an example of this type of violence. While Ahasuerus and Esther provide us with no direct solutions, the passage points us toward the providence of God. God was present with Esther during the king's outbursts and God is present with us today in the midst of all the violence and rage in our world. We must trust that, with God's presence and help, we will someday be ruled by peace.

My Prayer for Today:

Forgive the Words of My Mouth

"If you try my heart, if you visit me by night, if you test me, you will find no wickedness in me: my mouth does not transgress."

PSALM 17:3

Today's Prayer

Dear God, I pray for forgiveness of my transgressions and for the strength to obey your will. Amen.

Today's Reflection

I have a friend who gave up complaining for Lent; more specifically, she gave up complaining about others. This is a very noble and difficult Lenten discipline, especially if viewed in light of what the psalmist says, that even if God tests the heart and visits at night, God will find no transgressions of the mouth.

It is common for us to talk and complain about each other. Our home, workplaces, communities, and churches are full of gossips and complainers. The psalmist is asking for a clean heart and mouth. Realizing that we are human and subject to mistakes, the psalmist addresses a powerful and loving God, confident in God's merciful promise to forgive our transgressions and to remember them no more.

My Prayer for Today:

Day 68

Hope against Fear

"So do not be afraid; you are of more value than many sparrows."
MATTHEW 10:31

Today's Prayer

Thank you, Lord, for sending Christ to be our constant protection against the fears we face in our daily lives. Amen.

Today's Reflection

The sparrow is a small bird that often goes without notice. Yet Jesus reminds us that not even one sparrow goes without God's notice and God's protection.

Fear has one of the most life-draining effects on our human existence. We all face fear in our lives on a daily basis. Fear can affect all aspects of our life. Jesus reminds us that we are of more value than many sparrows to our God. God's presence and protection is with us continually, providing us with the assurance that God through Christ is our hope against fear.

My Prayer for Today:

Day 69

Called to Life

*"After this he went out and saw a tax collector named Levi,
sitting at the tax booth; and he said to him, 'Follow me.'
And he got up, left everything and followed him."*

LUKE 5:27–28

Today's Prayer

Lord, help me to discern your call and to become a faithful follower of Christ. Amen.

Today's Reflection

Notice the type of people Jesus calls; they are people like you and
me, people who represent a wide variety of lifestyles. In these verses,
Jesus calls a tax collector, a wealthy person with little respect from
the community. The people disliked tax collectors because they
worked for the Romans, and they cheated their own people to gain
wealth. When asked why he associated with people like this, Jesus
said he came not just to the righteous but to everyone. Jesus calls all
of us to be disciples of Christ, to follow the Christ who came to bring
us life—and not just life, but life abundant. It is very comforting to
know that you are included in this call to life.

My Prayer for Today:

Day 70

Being Part of the Family

"And you belong to Christ and Christ belongs to God."
1 CORINTHIANS 3:23

Today's Prayer

I give thanks to you, O Lord, for the gift of salvation through Jesus Christ. Amen.

Today's Reflection

Most psychologists would agree that having a sense of belonging is one of the most important factors in living a healthy life. My fondest memories are of growing up in a family where I felt loved and cared for, and I had a sense of belonging. That assurance gave me the things I needed to go out into a world where it's every person for himself. But even when we have that type of family, and there are many who don't, there will be times when life throws its curves and we will feel lost, alone, forgotten, and with no sense of belonging. It is at those times that the words of Paul bring me consolation. I'm consoled by the fact that, through Christ, I belong to God. That consolation gives me hope and joy.

My Prayer for Today:

Day 71

God Was Gracious to Sarah

*"The Lord dealt with Sarah as he has said, and the Lord
did for Sarah as he had promised."*
GENESIS 21:1

Today's Prayer

Gracious, all-knowing God, forgive me for the times when my
faith is weak and I, like Sarah, fail to believe your word. When I face
difficult situations, help me to remember that nothing is too hard for
you. Lord, this day, help me to trust you completely and not try to fix
it myself. Amen.

Today's Reflection

At any age, God's promises are true. And God's miraculous presence is seen and felt every day. A baby is born and we celebrate.
Miniature perfection, tiny nose, just enough fuzz to be called hair.
Ten perfect fingers and ten perfect toes. Sarah laughed at God's
promise that she would have a child. Too old? Not for God. Too
hard? Not for God. At any age, God's promises are true. That which
God promises, God is able to perform.

My Prayer for Today:

Who Am I?

*"But Moses said to God, 'Who am I that I should go to
Pharaoh, and bring the Israelites out of Egypt?' "*
EXODUS 3:11

Today's Prayer

O Great and Everlasting God, the God of our forebears, I come to
you humble in heart and on bended knee to acknowledge your awesome power and wonder in this world and in my life. I ask that you
will use me as you see fit and empower me to do your will. Amen.

Today's Reflection

"Who am I?" Moses asked God before performing this mighty
task. I am sure Rosa Parks asked, "Who am I?" two months before
she refused to go any farther back on the bus. "Who am I?" Martin
Luther King Jr. asked when, as a young minister, he was asked to
lead the Montgomery Bus Boycott.

Moses raises a second question: "Who are you?" God responded,
"I AM WHO I AM." When I go in God's name, it doesn't matter who
I am, because "I AM WHO I AM" is going with us. God will never as-
sign a task to us that we cannot accomplish because it is not "who I
am" that matters but rather that "I AM WHO I AM" is there with us.

My Prayer for Today:

If It Pleases the King

". . . and Esther rose and stood before the king."
ESTHER 8:5

Today's Prayer

Lord, when I fail to invite you into my plans and my decision making, life seems hard and thoughts overwhelm me. When I attempt to do anything without your favor, the simplest task becomes difficult. If it pleases the King, I pray your favor upon my life as you favored Esther. "Favor, my King," is what I stand in need of. For with your favor I will be able to do all that is required of me this day. Amen.

Today's Reflection

Have you ever asked someone to do a favor for you? I have, and it usually works out fine. Especially if the end results are what I anticipated. The favor is done and you move on. Have you ever asked God for favor? It's extraordinary. The end results are always more than you anticipated, even more than you could imagine. Doors seem to open that were closed, a resounding NO turns into an accommodating YES. People seem to be nicer to you because you walk in God's favor and even your enemies know it. I am blessed and highly favored.

My Prayer for Today:

Day 74

In My Distress I Cried to the Lord

"The Lord is my rock, my fortress, and my deliverer, my God, my rock in whom I take refuge, my shield, and the horn of my salvation, my stronghold."

PSALM 18:2

Today's Prayer

I love you, O Lord, my strength. Guide me as you guide the sunrise and direct the stars. Keep me in your holy, precious care as you care for the birds of the air and the lilies of the field. In my distress, shield my mind and guard my heart. Lord, I hurt. Hear me, help me, heal me. Lord, I've lost my way. Hear me, help me, guide me. Lord I need your guidance; hear me, help me, show me. Today, Lord, this hour, this moment, in my distress, hear me Lord, help me Lord, heal me Lord. Amen.

Today's Reflection

From the lion's den, God heard Daniel's prayer. When the Israelites cried out while in slavery, God heard and delivered. When my father died suddenly, something within me closed. When my sister died in her sleep, three years later, something within me cracked. But when my son died of suicide at age 26, my heart broke. In my distress I called to the Lord. I cried to my God for help. God heard me, God helped me, God healed me. There is no place we can be where God won't hear us. There is no situation so great that God can't help us. There is no sorrow too deep that God can't heal us. Today Lord, this hour, this moment, in my distress, hear me Lord, help me Lord, heal me Lord.

My Prayer for Today:

Day 75

The Kingdom Is Like . . .

"Listen! A sower went out to sow."
MATTHEW 13:3

Today's Prayer

Mysterious and Majestic God, thank you for the seed of your word that was planted in the soil of my heart many years ago. I pray your word will take root in me until it produces fruit that bears witness to your awesome love for me. Thank you for your kingdom, where my name has been changed from "sinner" to "saint" through the waters of my baptism. Lord, help me today to get past my issues. Help me, Lord, to remember that I am forgiven, justified, sanctified, and qualified to be in your kingdom by grace through faith, so that I may fully walk in your kingdom. Amen.

Today's Reflection

Jesus upset the apple cart. His kingdom rules seemed to be contrary to the religious laws that held the people hostage. Jesus was accused of disrespecting the Temple by healing on the Sabbath. There are times when we need to step out of the box of religiosity in order to walk more fully in the kingdom. The kingdom of God is the reign of God. The reign of God is the rule of God. Where God reigns there is peace, justice, and mercy for all. The demons of racism, classicism, ageism, and sexism are put on notice that the kingdom is near, and they tremble and flee. Jesus said the kingdom of God is within us. When we are nourished by the Word of God, the seed of faith takes root in the soil of our hearts. Then, the desire for justice, mercy, and peace becomes the way we live, act and treat one another.

My Prayer for Today:

Day 76

Disorder in the Church

"Do you not know that the saints will judge the world?"
1 CORINTHIANS 6:2

Today's Prayer

Loving God, help me to seek your will, your way, and your word when there appears to be irreconcilable disagreement in the church, or when I feel I have been wronged by a sister or brother. Help me to remember that your Word prescribes a way to handle disputes that differs from the world's legal systems. Amen.

Today's Reflection

The church is in the world (society), but not of the world. The church is called to be an example and a witness to the world. When the church, that is Christians, forget that we move to the beat of a different drummer (Scripture), disorder and chaos result. As Christians we have the Holy Spirit, the mind of Christ, and a law book (Scripture) to help us resolve conflict. Society has the legal system where disagreements are resolved in court with attorneys, judge, and jury. What image does the church give when Christians are taking Christians to secular court?

When we use the legal system of the world to resolve church issues, lawsuits make the church look bad and cause people to focus on its problems rather than its purpose. Christians are in the world to bear witness that the God we imitate is just, merciful, long suffering, and forgiving. Let us remember when conflict arises among Christians, instead of rushing to court, let us rush to our Christian law book and read Matthew 18:15–17, and act accordingly.

My Prayer for Today:

Blind from Birth: One Thing I Do Know, I Was Blind but Now I See.

"As he walked along, he saw a man blind from birth."
JOHN 9:1

Today's Prayer

O gracious, wonderful God, my redeemer, my salvation, my healer. Thank you for opening my eyes to see your blessings in my life. Forgive me, Lord, for complaining and whining when I relapse into moments of temporary blindness. Help me to trust you where I can't trace you. I magnify you, O awesome God. For you called me out of darkness into your marvelous light of new life, new joy, and new possibilities. Hallelujah to your name. This one thing I know—I once was blind but now I see. Hallelujah! Hallelujah! Amen.

Today's Reflection

Can you imagine the joy of an unexpected miracle? Blinded eyes opened. The man was born blind; he could see nothing. Then Jesus came by and the miraculous happened. Jesus put a mud patch on his eyes and told him to go wash in the pool of Siloam. The blind man did as Jesus said and he was healed. He could see. This incident created no small stir. We, too, were born blind. Blind to God's will, blind to God's way, blind to God's word. Blind to our need for salvation—until we accepted Christ as our Savior. In the waters of baptism, we were cleansed and given a new life. The scales of self-centeredness dropped from our eyes and we saw the glory of God in our lives, our minds, our bodies, and our affairs. We once were blind, but now we see. Praise God! Praise God! Praise God!

My Prayer for Today:

The Lord Will Provide

"On the mount of the Lord it shall be provided."
GENESIS 22:14

Today's Prayer

Eternal God, your ways are not our ways, and your thoughts are not our thoughts. We often forget this when we find ourselves caught between the rocks and hard places of life. We focus on our discomfort instead of our faith in you. Thank you for showing us that there are no tight spaces where your Spirit cannot enter and no sore spots that your love cannot soothe. In those times when what we face seems too difficult, assure us once again that you have a ram in the bush for every situation. Amen.

Today's Reflection

Abraham's faith is sorely tested by God's request to sacrifice his son Isaac. A request of this magnitude may not be made of us. However, there are issues and circumstances outside of the realm of the holy that put our faith, our patience, our sanity, and even our purse strings to the test. In life we will be tested—there's no way around it—but as Christians we endure, we go through, and we triumph with trust and faith in God who will provide.

My Prayer for Today:

Please Send Someone Else

"Oh my Lord, please send someone else."
EXODUS 4:13

Today's Prayer

Our Creator and Sustainer, the very idea that you would call us into service is often overwhelming. It is such a privilege, and yet the responsibility is awesome. Help us not to fear those things that you would lead us to do if we keep our eyes on your divine purpose instead of our human frailties. Lord, work through our fears and insecurities so that we may faithfully serve you and be a blessing to others. Amen.

Today's Reflection

Moses was a bit reluctant to say the least. Sound familiar? Has God asked you to go where you would rather not go and do what you would rather not do? Do you feel that you just don't have what it takes to meet the challenge, lead the charge, or answer the call? God not only calls us into service, God equips. The request that we most fear from God may well be a defining moment, the turning point, the way out of no way, or the ultimate blessing. Be of good courage. This is why God reminds us that what is important is not what we can do but rather what God can and will do through us.

My Prayer for Today:

Day 80

Uprooting Fear

*"All doing the king's work helped the Jews because the fear
of Mordecai fell upon them."*
ESTHER 9:3

Today's Prayer

Mighty God, let us remember that there will be times when we must diligently confront unrighteousness. Keep us mindful of all of your people and those who still struggle for the ordinary freedoms we take for granted. Let us know, Lord, that we always have you with us as an ally against evil. We thank you for your power and your protection. Amen.

Today's Reflection

Mordecai may well have been the Dr. Martin Luther King Jr. of his day. This story of Esther, the Jews, and King Ahasuerus is still a profound one for us. It's about a people's right to freedom, helping those who exist under oppression, and holding the oppressors accountable. It shows that a person can become the recipient of unexpected blessings. Mordecai sought the well-being of his people and rose to prominence not by blind ambition, but by the hand of God.

My Prayer for Today:

God Fulfills Our Desires

"You have given him his heart's desire."
PSALM 21:2

Today's Prayer

Oh God, how good it is to know that you are a God who hears and answers prayer. In our silence when words refuse to come, you are aware of the deep rumblings of our soul. In our anguish you comfort us, in our joy you lift us up! When we place our petitions upon your altar, you respond, you bless, you encourage. Thank you for bringing us peace and comfort in knowing that you lovingly give us the desires of our hearts. Amen.

Today's Reflection

When was the last time you had a praise report? God delivered you from a situation, blessed you with an opportunity, helped you mend a broken relationship, or just granted you a great day? Surely every time we breathe there is something to be grateful to God for. Why not take a moment out of each day, in fact right now, to identify one thing that God has done for you and then . . . PRAISE GOD!

My Prayer for Today:

What Is in Your Heart

*"But what comes out of the mouth proceeds from the heart,
and this is what defiles."*

MATTHEW 15:18

Today's Prayer

Gracious God, be patient with our human misinterpretations and values in the name of what is holy. Some have false notions but are well-meaning, hard-working servants. By your Spirit, Lord, show us that love and compassion are the keys to your heart and your kingdom. Amen.

Today's Reflection

What makes one holy? If you took a survey, everyone would have a different answer. Some of us think it's what you wear and don't wear, where you go and don't go, who you associate with or who you avoid. Others think it is certain church practices or activities. Still others will say it is consistent prayer and Bible study. Jesus gets to the heart of the matter. If one is sincere and attempting to live the Christian life with integrity, then they will know that we are Christians by our love. Our words will reflect our purity of spirit. We will think about, care for, and treat others with respect for their humanity. It's okay to try to do all of the right things, but it is better to develop true character and live in the right way. This is God's commandment, that you love one another, as God has loved you.

My Prayer for Today:

Day 83

Growing with God

"In whatever condition you were called, brothers and sisters, there remain with God."

1 CORINTHIANS 7:24

Today's Prayer

God, your infinite patience knows no bounds. You see us just as we are. You know our thoughts before we think them. You have even numbered the hairs on our heads. Each and every one of us has significance and meaning in your sight. You embrace us as is, warts, scars, and all. You see in us what others cannot see and what we have yet to discern within ourselves. We ask you, heavenly parent, that even though you accept us as we are, please continue to work your will in us so that we may become all that you need us to be. Amen.

Today's Reflection

We seem to forget that our spirituality and our relationship with God are two commitments that are enriched and developed over time. No one accepts Christ one day and is perfected the next. If you remain faithful, there will be a process of continuous growth. The good news is that God is willing to aid us in our development by gently, patiently, and lovingly fashioning us into worthy vessels.

My Prayer for Today:

Getting Away

"Jesus went up on a mountain by himself to pray."
MATTHEW 14:23

Today's Prayer

Heavenly Spirit, there are so many different ways we try to connect with you. Like Elijah we look for you in the wind, in the fire, and in the earthquake. Sometimes the best way to show you that we care is to spend some one-on-one time with you. God, may we be able to do that in order to be closer to you . . . there are times when we must be with you. Amen.

Today's Reflection

Go away! That's right, go away. Just go away, I said. Go away from the phone, the television, the game, the CD player, whatever and whoever is occupying your space and energy. It really is okay . . . after all, Jesus did it. Between twelve disciples, multitudes of people, powers, principalities, and Pharisees, he needed time. Time to regroup, recharge, reflect, to hear and understand his instructions and his purpose from the heavenly one. Occasionally, the most meaningful way to reach, be with, hear from, and to know God, is to just go away.

My Prayer for Today:

Day 85

Pray Expecting

*"Isaac prayed to the Lord for his wife, because she was
barren: and the Lord granted his prayer, and his wife
Rebekah conceived."*
GENESIS 25:21

Today's Prayer

Creator God, author of life, I thank you for the special love between husbands and wives. Please be with those couples who desire
to have children but are experiencing infertility difficulties. Hear
their prayer and answer them in the precious name of Jesus. Amen.

Today's Reflection

Genesis 25:20 tells us that Isaac married Rebekah at age 40, and
that Rebekah was having problems conceiving. In biblical times a
woman's identity was tied to being someone's wife and mother. If a
wife was unable to have children, she was labeled "barren," which
was considered a curse. Isaac loved Rebekah and he prayed on her
behalf that God would grant her mercy. God heard Isaac's prayer and
Rebekah conceived and gave birth to twin sons Esau and Jacob.
There is power in intercessory prayer. When we are asked to pray for
one another, the request must be taken seriously because someone is
depending on a blessing from the Lord.

My Prayer for Today:

Do You Care?

"Since I first came to Pharaoh to speak in your name, he has mistreated this people, and you have done nothing at all to deliver your people."

EXODUS 5:23

Today's Prayer

God of mercy, I thank you for being God almighty! I pray that you build up with courage and strength your messengers who advocate for the poor and powerless in our society. Amen.

Today's Reflection

Moses and Aaron dared to confront the Egyptian slave system. They faced Pharaoh directly, asking on behalf of the enslaved Israelites for their release from hard labor, and the opportunity to worship God freely in the wilderness. However, their request was not only denied, but the Israelites received an additional amount of hard labor! Moses was angry with God. He felt that God had mistreated the people because their situation grew worse instead of better. We need to remember that when our situations in life seem to get worse, we can be real with God and tell God our true feelings, too.

My Prayer for Today:

A Caring Leader

*"For Mordecai the Jew was next in rank to King
Ahasuerus, and he was powerful among the Jews and popular with his many kindred, for he sought the good of his
people and interceded for the welfare of all his
descendants."*

ESTHER 10:3

Today's Prayer

God of justice and liberation, I thank you for your servant Mordecai, a man who loved his community to the point of risking his own life on their behalf. Help me to develop this same type of passion and love for my community. Amen.

Today's Reflection

Mordecai, who was a Jew, didn't keep silent! Once he learned about the plot to massacre all the Jews in the country, he got busy to stop this evil plan. He boldly approached Queen Esther, who was also a Jew in the King's Court. He reminded her who she was, and that the plot to destroy the Jewish community included her as well. Mordecai helped Queen Esther to see that her position "was for such a time as this" to save her people from mass destruction. Mordecai's love for his community saved their lives. God calls all of us to love our community and to be an advocate for the poor and oppressed. One person can help to make a difference.

My Prayer for Today:

Day 88

Alone?

"My God, my God, why have you forsaken me?"
PSALM 22:1

Today's Prayer

Precious Lord, I thank you for being there for me when I feel alone and discouraged. If you turn away from me what would I do? Never leave or forsake me because without you I can't make it. Amen.

Today's Reflection

"My God, why have you forsaken me?" Jesus asked this question to God while he was dying on the Cross. Have you ever felt forsaken by God? Was it because of an unanswered prayer request, or because God failed to change a situation in your favor? Psalm 22 shows us clearly that we are encouraged to come to the Lord just as we are with our pain, disappointments, and fears. We serve a loving God who desires to be part of our everyday lives.

My Prayer for Today:

Do You Know?

"He said to them, 'But who do you say that I am?'"
MATTHEW 16:15

Today's Prayer

Lord Jesus, thank you for making yourself available to me. Help me to be a bold witness about who you are to me. Let me not be afraid to tell somebody how you changed me and claimed me as your own. This I ask in your name. Amen.

Today's Reflection

Jesus asked his disciples, who did they say he was? They were the closest people to him on a daily basis. They were the ones who were present at all of the miracles, healings, and other signs and wonders. They were the ones who witnessed how the religious establishment tried to discredit his authority because he dared to challenge their interpretation of the law. Yes, Jesus wanted to know if the disciples knew who was in their midst. Peter identified Jesus as the Messiah, the Son of the living God. Jesus gave hope and new life to all he encountered. Who do you say Jesus is? Is he your friend, one you can depend on? Can you say that he is your Savior and redeemer? You are given the invitation to know Jesus for yourself; will you accept?

My Prayer for Today:

Day 90

Doing What It Takes

*"To the weak I became weak, so that I might win the weak.
I have become all things to all people, that I might by all
means save some. I do it all for the sake of the gospel, so
that I may share in its blessings."*
1 CORINTHIANS 9:22–23

Today's Prayer

Creator God, thank you for identifying with each human condition. You are always reaching out to your children who are the poor in society. Help me to walk with the orphans, people who are homeless, people living with AIDS, and others who are excluded in our society. Amen.

Today's Reflection

In Paul's letter to the Corinthians he identifies himself as an apostle of the gospel. Not only has Paul dedicated his life in spreading the good news of Jesus Christ, he also makes it relevant to the community he is serving. By relating to personal conditions or circumstances that people experience, he is able to demonstrate that Jesus cares about all of our issues. There is nothing too bad or shameful that Jesus can't fix.

My Prayer for Today:

God's Love

"So we have known and believe the love that God has for us. God is love, and those who abide in love abide in God and God abides in them."

1 JOHN 4:16

Today's Prayer

God of love, thank you for your abiding presence in my life. Thank you for always dwelling with me. I know that you love me because you gave your only Son to die for me. Continue to keep your Holy Spirit in me, so all who see your love will be drawn to you. Amen.

Today's Reflection

Do you know that you are loved today? You are loved because of God's Holy Spirit that abides within you. Sometimes because of life's hardships and struggles it may be hard to believe that God is with you. However, we are reminded in 1 John 4:16 that God is love and God's love abides in us. The challenge we face is, will we abide with God?

My Prayer for Today:

Day 92

Lord, Is That You?

"And that very night the Lord appeared to him and said, 'I am God of your father Abraham.' "
GENESIS 26:23

Today's Prayer

Lord God, you are truly amazing! I thank you for loving and caring for me in spite of my faults. Help me to love others as you love me. Speak to me, God, speak to me. Amen.

Today's Reflection

The writer of Genesis tells us in no uncertain terms that the Lord appeared to Isaac and told him exactly what to do. How many times have we prayed for God to speak so plainly? We have a longing for dramatic communication from God, in Red Sea fashion! God, speak to me.

My Prayer for Today:

Day 93

God Is Yet Able

". . . they would not listen to Moses, because of their broken spirit and their cruel slavery."
EXODUS 6:9

Today's Prayer

Merciful God, sustainer of all that is, help me to believe in your promises of grace when my spirit sags, my soul aches, and the cares of life threaten to overshadow your love for me. Be near to all who are brokenhearted this day, let us see the light of your will for our lives. In the precious name of Jesus, I pray. Amen.

Today's Reflection

God commanded Moses to tell the Israelites that freedom was on its way. Prayers answered! Deliverance! Freedom! This was good news! Misery had become a part of the Israelites' daily lives for so many years they could not believe God's message of liberation above the racket of their "broken spirit and their cruel slavery." In many respects we are no different. God's voice becomes muffled beneath the weight of our sagging, sore spirits and the screaming pain of our circumstances. We get so embroiled in our situations that we can forget that God is near. But if we dare to hope and meet God in prayer, we find, like the Israelites, that despite our pains, betrayals and circumstances, God is yet able to save, deliver, and set us free.

My Prayer for Today:

Lord, Do Something!

"Why do you make me see wrongdoing and look at trouble?"

HABAKKUK 1:3

Today's Prayer

Praise you, God, for the gift of sight, and being able to see both the beautiful and the wretched. We thank you for empowering us to mend the brokenness of our communities through Jesus Christ our savior and brother. Amen.

Today's Reflection

Daily we see all manner of destruction, wrongdoing, violence, and trouble. The skeletal remains of abandoned houses dot the landscapes of our urban centers. The AIDS epidemic is attacking African Americans at an alarming rate. Our children are no longer safe in school. Lord, do something! God, "sic 'em," we scream. This is exactly what the prophet Habakkuk did: "Why do I have to see wrongdoing and trouble! Destruction and violence are before me." The prophet's desperate cry, like ours, is "Lord, do something—anything!" But God has done something. God has acted decisively in our baptisms and calls us to "do something." What God calls us to do, God equips us to handle. So get active in church, find a ministry or engage in a cause to help alleviate suffering. It is your turn—now go do something!

My Prayer for Today:

Day 95

For the Chronically Ill

"The Lord is my shepherd."
PSALM 23:1

Today's Prayer

Merciful Father, we lift before you those who are chronically ill. Wrap them in your embrace and assure them of your love, care, and protection. In Jesus' name, I pray. Amen.

Today's Reflection

We usually hear Psalm 23 at funerals, but the "shepherd's psalm" also gives assurance of God's love and protection in the face of chronic illness.

As a pastor, I visited the homebound members in the congregation. One day I visited two women. First, I saw one who had had a severe stroke and was barely able to speak. Through tears, she cried, asking God, "Why?" Why the stroke, why did her husband have to die? After her lament, in her warbled speech, she recited Psalm 23. Despite her frustration, she was assured of God's care for her.

Later that afternoon, I saw another Mother of the Church; she was in the late stages of Alzheimer's disease. Her caregiver led her into the kitchen and planted her at the table. She had a faraway look in her eyes. As I prepared communion, a look of recognition came over her face. In a moment of absolute clarity, she said, "The Lord is my shepherd."

Two different women: one imprisoned by her body and one imprisoned by her mind and yet both find comfort in God's word.

My Prayer for Today:

For Reconciliation in the Church

"If another member of the church sins against you."
MATTHEW 18:15

Today's Prayer

Gracious Lord, we thank you for the gift of church on earth and life together in our congregation. Teach us to live out the ministry of reconciliation with each other and the world. In Jesus' name. Amen.

Today's Reflection

There are no folks like church folks. We worship together on Sundays. Some of our richest relationships are with our sisters and brothers in church. When a church member experiences a death in the family, there is an outpouring of concern. We celebrate the critical moments in our lives in the context of the church: baptism, confirmation, and marriage. While we know how to do "church" well, we tend not to handle the simplest of misunderstandings well. Misunderstandings can churn into a full-scale "church fight" which can leave hurt feelings in its wake.

"If another member of the church sins against you, go and point it out when the two of you are alone," Jesus tells us. Don't complain to Sister "so-and-so." Go to that brother or sister under cover of prayer and in the spirit of Christ, then speak from the heart, with the highest hope that reconciliation will take place. Paul tells us (2 Corinthians 5:18) that each of us has been called to the ministry of reconciliation. Who are you holding a grudge against? Try your hand at reconciliation today; it's what we're called to do!

My Prayer for Today:

For the Spirit of Generosity

*"Truly I tell you, that this poor widow has given more than
all of them."*

LUKE 21:3

Today's Prayer

Lord God, giver of every gift, we thank you for blessing us with
the gift of life and breath. All that we have comes from you; stir up in
us the spirit of generosity to support the mission of the church at
home and in the world. In Jesus' name. Amen.

Today's Reflection

During my pastoral internship in India, the story of the poor widow
came alive. One Sunday, toward the middle of worship, a woman
walked into church. Her sari was clean but threadbare as gauze. I
watched her make her way through the pews, careful to find a seat—
for it is considered improper for a single woman to sit next to a man
she doesn't know. She found a seat near a few older women like herself.

During the offering of thanksgiving, she gave a generous offering
of five rupees (Indian dollars) in the collection plate. As she gave her
offering, she softly spoke. I turned toward the interpreter. "She said,
she thanks God for her many blessings and life." Shortly before
the benediction, she quietly slipped out. Curiosity got the best of
me. As soon as worship was over, I hurried out to follow her.
Down the street, she found her place on the curb and sat down.
This woman was a beggar! She lived on the streets, yet she gave an
offering with thanksgiving. I probably will never see this woman
again, but she challenges all of us not to give to the church out of

our abundance but to give of our "first fruits" for the building of
the realm of God.

My Prayer for Today:

The Eucharist

*"For as often as you eat this bread and drink the cup, you
proclaim the Lord's death until he comes."*

1 CORINTHIANS 11:26

Today's Prayer

Merciful God, we praise you for every opportunity to feast at your
holy table. May this gift continue to nourish us, heal us, empower us
through your Son, Jesus the Christ. Amen.

Today's Reflection

What a holy mystery we share in the Eucharist! Eucharist is true
"soul food." In it we are nourished and strengthened for the
Christian journey for all time and eternity. We bring our brokenness
to draw from Jesus' boundless grace and mercy. Reconciliation,
restoration, healing, and forgiveness are found there.

In the Eucharist, divisions of time and eternity are bridged. As we
gather around the table, so does a great cloud of witnesses from
every time and age. I was reluctant to take an extended trip because
I was afraid that my very aged grandmother would die while I was
away. I told her of my fear. She smiled and said, "I don't intend to die
while you are away, but in any case, if the Lord comes for me, I will
just see you next Sunday at the communion table." Thank you God
for your precious gift of Eucharist and for the wisdom of the older
saints.

My Prayer for Today:

Blessed Before the Lord

"Bring me game, and prepare for me savory food to eat,
that I may bless you before the Lord before I die."

GENESIS 27:7

Today's Prayer

Holy One, we thank you for the young people in our lives. They are your gift to us for the future. We ask that you would bless them richly. Help them to dream big dreams and to achieve them. Keep them safe from the dangers around every corner. Grant them longevity and prosperity. Fill their lives with the richness of your presence and never leave them alone. For Christ's sake. Amen.

Today's Reflection

In this story of sibling rivalry and betrayal, Isaac prepares to bless his oldest son. Tradition emphasizes Jacob's deceit. However, we should not overlook the example set by Isaac; he prayed that the Lord would bless his child.

In recent years we have been inundated with reports describing our young people as lost and predicting that they are the first generation who will not do as well as their parents. In this era, Isaac's example resounds. We need to lift our youth up to the Lord and ask our God to bless them richly. Any success that we have had is in part because our mothers and fathers, grandmothers and grandfathers stayed on their knees before the Lord for us. Perhaps it's time we went down on our knees for the next generation.

My Prayer for Today:

A God of Action

"The Egyptians shall know that I am the Lord."

EXODUS 7:5

Today's Prayer

Holy One, I thank you that you are a God of action. You have not left me to suffer alone or to struggle by myself. Whenever I have been in need, you have been with me, working out the details behind the scenes. Help me to rely completely on you. In Jesus' name. Amen.

Today's Reflection

The Lord is fed up! God gave Pharaoh a sign to encourage him to send the Hebrews forth, but Pharaoh would not be persuaded. It was then that the Lord set the plagues in motion that would lead to the eventual liberation of the Hebrews enslaved in Egypt. "Thus says the Lord, 'By this you shall know that I am the Lord.'" It was not enough for the Lord to tell Pharaoh; God had to show him that there were consequences for defying his will. Isn't it good to know that God is not just a God of words, but of action? God is actively at work on our behalf, making a way for us behind the scenes, planning our way of escape. Whatever you are going through, know that the Lord will stretch out a hand to bring you out. By this you will know that he is the Lord.

My Prayer for Today:

Silence in the Storm

*"The Lord is in his holy temple; let all the earth keep
silence before him!"*

HABAKKUK 2:20

Today's Prayer

Holy One, I am silent before you. Speak to me your will and embolden me to live it out in the world today. When the world's troubles threaten to overtake me, lead me back to your throne and help me find my peace in you. In Jesus' name. Amen.

Today's Reflection

It is perplexing that Habakkuk utters words of peace in this chapter. Amid the noise produced by injustice in the world, false gods vying for Israel's attention, and the cataclysmic destruction that the prophet foretells, he ends this chapter with a plea for reverent silence.

But this call for reverent silence should not take us by surprise. We experience such cacophony every day in our busy lives. The storm of deafening noise in our world does not relent for our times of devotion. Yet as we seek the Lord amid the clamor, we can find the peaceful eye of the storm in the Lord's sweet presence. When the noise of this world threatens to overwhelm you, return to that quiet space found only in God.

My Prayer for Today:

Day 102

An Uplifted Soul

"To you, O Lord, I lift up my soul."
PSALM 25:1

Today's Prayer

Holy One, I lift my soul to you. Holy One, I raise and hold myself before you. Holy One, I bear myself before you. Holy One, I lay bare my soul before you with all my vulnerabilities, weaknesses, and faults. I am naked before your penetrating gaze. Stripped of the masks I hide behind, my veneer removed, I stand exposed. Search me, Lord, from my skin to my sin deep within. "For your name's sake, O Lord, pardon my guilt, for it is great." Make me whole as you are whole. To your whole, knit my soul and live anew in me. For Christ's sake I pray. Amen.

Today's Reflection

In God's presence, we find renewal and transformation. Imagine if we began each day of our life raising our souls up to God, asking the Lord to renew us, and requesting a fresh anointing of the Holy Spirit. Imagine if we began each day with a prayer reaffirming our utter trust in the Lord. How would that transform our interaction with our families and coworkers? How would that transform our daily witness? How would that transform our world? As you engage in the activities of the day, keep your soul lifted up, in constant communion with Christ, and see how it transforms you.

My Prayer for Today:

Blessed Anyhow

"Am I not allowed to do what I choose with what belongs to me? Or are you envious because I am generous?"
MATTHEW 20:15

Today's Prayer

Holy One, I come before you confessing my enviousness. I have envied the good fortune that you have granted to others. I have taken for granted the way you have blessed me. Help me to recount today the many blessings you have given me in spite of who I am, what I have done, and what I have left undone. Thank you for being extraordinarily generous to me. In Jesus' name. Amen.

Today's Reflection

What a peculiar thing is God's grace. The blessings that flow from on high are available to everyone. In fact, the Lord makes the "sun rise on the evil and on the good, and sends rain on the righteous and on the unrighteous" (Matthew 5:25). How easy it would be to begrudge our brothers for the blessings they get and to hold our sisters' good fortune against them because we believe we are more deserving; we have worked harder, struggled longer, and been more faithful than they have. Yet, they are being blessed anyhow.

Perhaps that's when we should remember that we are also unworthy: "Our righteous deeds are like filthy cloth" (Isaiah 64:6). There is nothing we can do to earn God's grace. So let us rejoice that God blesses us anyhow.

My Prayer for Today:

Using Our Gifts for the Church

"So with yourselves; since you are eager for spiritual gifts, strive to excel in them for building up the church."

1 CORINTHIANS 14:12

Today's Prayer

Holy One, I thank you for the gifts that you have placed in me. I recognize that you have not given them to me for my own glorification, but for the edification of the body of Christ in this world. Use me, Lord! I (re)commit myself and my gifts to you, and wait anxiously to see how you will use me to help build your Church in this world. For Christ's sake. Amen.

Today's Reflection

Did you know you have charisma? As Christians we each have charisma, gifts that God has given to us. Although we each have them, they are not all the same. These gifts often find expression in the careers we have chosen, in the talents we possess, and in the activities we enjoy. But like every blessing, these gifts come with a responsibility. We are responsible to give these gifts back to the body of Christ and to use them to strengthen the Christian community. In this regard, we all have a ministry to which we are called. Have you discovered yours? Take some time today to entreat Christ to help you discern what your gifts are and how you can develop them. You and your gifts are important parts of God's plan of redemption. You may be surprised by what God has in store for you.

My Prayer for Today:

Walk in Love

"There was a man sent from God, whose name was John."
2 JOHN 1:6

Today's Prayer

Holy One, make your love real in me. Transform the way I treat others. Let your love unite where there is division, mend where there are fractures, and bring peace where there is strife. Grant me your power to love both my adversaries and my friends. Let someone see the light of your love in me and come to you. In Christ's name. Amen.

Today's Reflection

When Christ's commandments to us are described, they always come back to one issue: love. Love should move us to strive for justice for those who have been victimized, recompense for those who have been wronged, and harmony for those who are in conflict. It should circumscribe the way we treat each other; it should govern our behavior at all times.

But love is more than just a matter of behavior; love is a matter of character, defining who we are. The more we are submitted to Christ's will for our lives, the more this love expresses itself in us. Can people see Christ in you by the way you love those you interact with every day? Today, make it your goal to walk in love. Who knows, someone might find Christ because of God's love reflected through you.

My Prayer for Today:

When Enough Is Never Enough

"Esau went to Ishmael and took Mahalath daughter of Abraham's son Ishmael."

GENESIS 28:9

Today's Prayer

Dear God, forgive me for those times when I felt a need to win the respect of others by changing who I am. Amen.

Today's Reflection

Every society has expectations that accompany marriage. In ancient Israel, men were expected to marry their father's brother's daughter—a cousin. Ishmael married Canaanite women. To make up for marrying the wrong person and to win the favor of his parents, Esau took another wife—his father's brother's daughter (this was Mahalath, Ishmael's daughter). Yet, legally, this too was an incorrect marriage because Ishmael's mother was Hagar, a woman without status in the clan. Esau's effort to please his parents backfired. We know this because of the way the biblical story later unfolds.

Sometimes enough is never enough. We are pressured on all sides. If we do what others expect of us, we become people-pleasers, and this is a dead-end road. We should strive to understand and act on God's perspective. When we do that, it is always enough for God.

My Prayer for Today:

Courage to Confront a Hardened Heart

"Then the Lord said to Moses, 'Go to Pharaoh and say to him, "Thus says the Lord: Let my people go . . ."'"
EXODUS 8:1

Today's Prayer

Creator God, please grant me the courage to confront a person who abuses his authority and who has a hardened heart. I also pray for the wisdom to refrain from pleading with hardened hearts, unless you send me, as you sent Moses. Amen.

Today's Reflection

In chapter 8 we find an unquestioning Moses, a Moses who returns to Pharaoh knowing that he will refuse him. And yet, Moses returns anyhow, trusting that God is with him. God is with us, too. Today, God's Spirit is calling us to release people who are still bound by oppressive structures at home, at work, in the church, and in the world: "Let my women go!" "Let my children go!" "Let those who are homeless go!" "Let those who are ill go!" Let us trust that God will supply us with the courage and skills to confront hardened hearts, or to withhold our voices until God says speak.

My Prayer for Today:

Respecting God's Wrath

"I hear and tremble within; my lips quiver at the sound."
HABAKKUK 3:16

Today's Prayer

Dear God, when I am tempted the most, please help me to remember your love, as well as your wrath. Lead me in the way of righteousness. Amen.

Today's Reflection

We often emphasize God's mercy, steadfastness, loving-kindness, and blessings because God's wrath is so frightening. But today, let us take a moment to consider how enraged God becomes at unrepentant sin and injustice. The prophet Habakkuk said that he "trembles within." For a moment, let us tremble before our mighty and just God.

My Prayer for Today:

Day 109

God Will Not Forsake Us

*"If my father and mother forsake me, the Lord
will take me up."*

PSALM 27:10

Today's Prayer

Thank you, God, for sticking closer to me than any friend or relative. If I have unjustly forsaken someone, please reveal it to me, O Lord. Amen.

Today's Reflection

Sometimes the people closest to us turn away. Sometimes it is caused by our mistakes. Sometimes it is an error in communication. Sometimes we are dealing with an obstinate or judgmental personality. Whatever the case, it can feel extremely lonely and even devastating. It takes time to heal when loved ones forsake us. It takes time to learn to trust again. But in the meantime, the psalmist reminds us that God is always there waiting to take us up when human hands fail us. Indeed, like a loving parent takes on the needs of a child, the Lord will take you up.

My Prayer for Today:

Dealing with Critics

"Neither will I tell you by what authority I am doing these things."

MATTHEW 21:27

Today's Prayer

Dear God, I pray for the ability to deal wisely with those who criticize me, whether maliciously or from ignorance. Amen.

Today's Reflection

There are many episodes in Jesus' life that may instruct us in ours. For example, in Matthew 21, the chief priests and elders challenged Jesus' abilities and credentials. As African Americans, our credentials are often challenged. This can be a terrible burden in the workplace, in church, or in school. Yet Jesus understands and helps us because he knows exactly what that is like. How did Jesus respond to a question designed to trick him and get him into trouble? He responded with a question, and when the priests and elders could not answer, Jesus refused to answer them also. Is there a revelation in this for you that will help you at your job, home, or church? Jesus understands. Sometimes Jesus had such an unloving audience that he had to refuse to keep explaining himself, and sometimes we have to do the same.

My Prayer for Today:

Don't Let Anyone or Anything Turn You Around

"Therefore my beloved, be steadfast, immovable, always excelling in the work of the Lord . . ."
1 CORINTHIANS 15:58

Today's Prayer

O God, help me to remember that your son Jesus gives us strength and power to overcome. Amen.

Today's Reflection

O death, where is your victory? O unemployment, where is your victory? O divorce, where is your victory? O sickness, where is your victory? O infertility, where is your victory? O racism, where is your victory? O sexism, where is your victory? O drug addiction, where is your victory? O prison, where is your victory? Although we may have problems, and might not be able to figure out what God is doing in our lives, let none of these things turn us around. God has a plan for your life and mine, and God has already worked it out.

"This battle is not for you to fight . . . see the victory of the Lord on your behalf" (2 Chronicles 20:17). Therefore, "be steadfast, immovable, excelling . . . because you know you do not labor in vain."

My Prayer for Today:

Day 112

Supporting Christians

*"Therefore, we ought to support such people, so that we
may become coworkers with the truth."*

3 JOHN 8

Today's Prayer

Dear God, show me how to be supportive of those in ministry
who need my support. Amen.

Today's Reflection

John speaks of support that covers the basic needs someone must
have to engage in ministry without hindrance. Take a moment to reflect upon how you feel about supporting those in ministry. The av-
erage pastor or associate minister gives far more than he or she ever
receives. Often, pastors and ministers give out of their personal earn-
ings to families in need because some parishioners do not want to
open church coffers. John is trying to help us overcome any ten-
dency to withhold support. The assumption that John makes is that
we are supporting ministers, missionaries and pastors who are not
abusing the people or their trust in any way. Where there is abuse, it
is just to end support and redirect it until change has come. John
challenges us to find God's faithful servants who depend on us and
to give them our support so that the hopeful, healing, and liberating
power of God may go forward unhindered.

My Prayer for Today:

Divine Order

"May the Lord watch between you and me, when we are absent one from the other."

GENESIS 31:49

Today's Prayer

God of infinite wisdom, I trust you to always care for me and to guide me along the pathways of my life. I confess that I am often confused by the events and circumstances I encounter. I can't always explain why things happen, nor do I understand why I make the choices that I do. Grant me your gifts of good judgment, and give me confidence that all things in my life will work for good, according to your will. Amen.

Today's Reflection

Things are not always as they appear. I have learned this the hard way. People have deceived me, and I have deceived others. Why does dishonesty often seem to be the easy way out of my problems? I am so often tempted to be less than truthful, especially in my personal life. I call upon God's power today to fill me with the courage to both tell the truth and to recognize the truth in what others say to me. Watch over me, God, so that the truth will set me free.

My Prayer for Today:

What God Can Do

*"This is why I have let you live: to show you my power, and
to make my name resound through all the earth."*
EXODUS 9:16

Today's Prayer

Praise the Lord, who can do all things and who does all things
well. Praise the God who made heaven and earth, the God who
made me and continues to keep me alive. Praise the Creator who will
give life to my dreams and joy to my heart this day. Hear my prayer
of praise today, God Almighty. Amen.

Today's Reflection

As I read about Moses and Pharaoh, I wonder how someone could
be so stubborn. God had to do awful things to Pharaoh and his people to make them free their slaves. Am I this stubborn toward God?
What does God want me to do differently? What changes do I need
to make in my life? Today I will open myself up to God's messages to
me. With the help of God, I will stop turning away from God's word
to me. Speak now, Lord, in the way that is best for me to hear from
you. Your servant is listening.

My Prayer for Today:

Day 115

A Brand New Me

"Be strong, and let your heart take courage, all you who wait for the Lord."
PSALM 31:24

Today's Prayer

Jesus, Master, Guardian of my soul, hear my prayer. Let your strong Spirit fill me today with courage and strength, so that I may follow you and serve you. You know that I am often impatient with myself. I confess that I have also been impatient with you. Reveal to me the wisdom of your plan for my life. I trust you to show me what to do and when to do it, even if today is a day that I need do nothing but wait on you. Amen.

Today's Reflection

Martin Luther King Jr. once wrote about the strength that people need in order to truly love each other. He knew that this kind of strength was often hidden in the character of people whose lives were marked by suffering and injustice. I know people who have this kind of strength. They resist the temptation to return evil for evil. They combat violence with a spirit of peace. They are not weak, nor are they fools. Today they remind me that I have something important to accomplish with the strength that God has given me. Today I will be strong for God and of service to someone else.

My Prayer for Today:

Day 116

The Sankofa Invitation

*"I will restore your judges as at the first, and your
counselors as at the beginning."*
ISAIAH 1:26

Today's Prayer

Ancient and Invisible One, my prayers today celebrate your power
which was made known to my ancestors. I thank you for your presence with them and your faithfulness to them. I praise you for the
greatness of my people's history. May I never forget the testimony of
past generations, for through their stories I learn so much more about
you. You are the same yesterday, today, and forever. Hallelujah and
Amen.

Today's Reflection

Sankofa is a concept from West Africa that invites me to use the
best wisdom and traditions of the past as my foundation for the future. Sankofa teaches me to cherish the lessons of history and remember the truth that has already been revealed. Sankofa also connects
me to the ancestors who lived before me and lifts them up as evidence
of my own potential. I am somebody because I come from a proud
and noble people. Let me honor them today in all that I say, do, and
believe.

My Prayer for Today:

Have I Forgotten Something?

"Give therefore to the emperor the things that are the emperor's, and to God the things that are God's."

MATTHEW 22:21

Today's Prayer

God my provider, everything I have comes from you. You have given me the gift of life itself, and you support me with all the blessings I find in my community. Teach me to be more like you by becoming a more generous person. Show me how to share with those who are in need, and in so doing let me give honor to you. Amen.

Today's Reflection

If I were to write down everything I need to do today, would I include those things I need to do for God? The Bible is filled with wisdom reminding me that God expects something from me. God wants me to work for justice, to serve others, and to maintain a personal life that is morally and physically healthy. God also wants me to take time out for prayer. These actions can take many forms, but they must be done joyfully. Let me live today in thanksgiving to the God who is everything to me.

My Prayer for Today:

Day 118

Continuing to Rise

*"Indeed, we felt that we had received the sentence of death
so that we would not rely on ourselves but on God who
raises the dead."*
2 CORINTHIANS 1:9

Today's Prayer

God of new life, you have never known defeat. Your power is always available, and your Spirit is always at work. Be at work in my life today, especially in the circumstances that are so discouraging to me right now. Teach me again that even in the midst of my personal failures, you can show me the victory of faith, hope, and love. Amen.

Today's Reflection

No matter what obstacles are placed in my path and no matter what emotional pain causes me to suffer, I have a confident attitude about myself and my potential. I do not foolishly deny that I face very serious challenges. I see these challenges every day, but my spirit sees much more. My spirit sees the power of God that was revealed when Jesus was raised from the dead. I am God's child, too, and I, too, will rise today.

My Prayer for Today:

Sad But True

"They are waterless clouds carried along by the winds;
autumn trees without fruit, twice dead, uprooted."
JUDE 12

Today's Prayer

Giver of divine direction, you are able to guide me through the maze of voices and choices and influences that confuse and disturb my life. You continue to teach me to be careful in how I live and to be wise in choosing friends. Let your wisdom take control of me today, so that I will walk along a path that is pleasing to you. Keep me from evil and fill me with your goodness. Amen.

Today's Reflection

When I was a boy, my father used to say, "When the crowd goes this way, you go that way." My father was warning me about the seductive ways of careless living. The things that bring shame into our lives often appear to be popular and exciting. How easy it is for me to assume that just because everybody else is doing something it must be all right. I thank God for my father's wisdom. Sometimes, I need to remember the counsel of wise people who know that if I am to reach my God-given potential, some things and some people are better left alone.

My Prayer for Today:

Holding On

"But Jacob said, 'I will not let you go, unless you bless me.'"
GENESIS 32:26

Today's Prayer

God, you have promised that you would bless me and provide for me. Help me to be confident while you are moving on my behalf. Help me not to be anxious or unsettled, but instead give me the courage to wait until you bless me. Amen.

Today's Reflection

Often, we find ourselves desperately seeking a blessing from God. It can be for improved health, financial gain, or relationship restoration. To be sure, it is right for us to turn to God for God to meet our need; God is our provider. But there is also an attitude that can prepare us to fully access what God has for us. This posture encourages us to determine that regardless of what things look like, we will not give up faith or hope. We will continue to hold on to God until our blessing is realized.

My Prayer for Today:

Day 121

The Worth of the Word

*"The tablets were the work of God, and the writing was the
writing of God, engraved upon the tablets."*
EXODUS 32:16

Today's Prayer

Thank you, God, for giving me instruction on how to serve and
worship you. Thanks for not leaving me to my own devices and personal agenda. Show me how to honor your word with a life that
gives witness to your direction. Amen.

Today's Reflection

Sometimes we forget that there are some things that we don't have
to personally ponder, figure out, or even fully understand. God has
already given us direction and revelation through the life-giving
power of God's Word. Indeed, the commandments of the Bible are
the very work of God, written for us so that we might continue along
the path of spiritual maturity and development. Without a doubt, the
Word is priceless. It is not simply for our information; instead the Word
has been given to form and shape us.

My Prayer for Today:

Free to Fail

*"Happy are those whose transgression is forgiven, whose
sin is covered."*

PSALM 32:1

Today's Prayer

Lord, I pray for those held hostage by a fixation with perfection.
Give them strength to face their sins. Help them, and me, to receive
your grace. Amen.

Today's Reflection

In a competitive society, it is easy to fall prey to the widely pervasive push to be better or best, if not perfect. Moreover, recognition
seems to be given to those who are either able to get through life
without significant error or who have mastered the ability to cover
up transgressions and shortcomings. But God suggests that happi-
ness is not lodged in perfection, but springs forth from our willing-
ness to acknowledge our sins. We can walk in joy when we realize
that God does not refuse to love us simply because we make a mistake. Indeed, God invites us to acknowledge our sins. We are free to
fail, because God's forgiveness is freely given.

My Prayer for Today:

Day 123

Faceless Faith

*"What do you mean by crushing my people, by grinding
the face of the poor? says the Lord God of hosts."*
ISAIAH 3:14

Today's Prayer

God of provision, I confess that I have ignored the cries and the
needs of your people. Sometimes it has been easy to walk past people who are homeless without even taking notice. Forgive me for not
seeing the faces of the oppressed. Help me to resist the evil of over-
consumption. And give me the strength to share the resources that
you have given us. Amen.

Today's Reflection

It is easy for us to get comfortable with all the material posses-
sions that we have. We are quick to enjoy the items that we have ac-
quired and hesitant to disguise our satisfaction. And sometimes this
becomes prideful arrogance. However, God reminds us that our in-
dulgence and fascination with goods is grinding the face of the poor.
As such, we must choose to give our faith a facelift. We are called to
make life choices that give witness to our oneness with all people.

My Prayer for Today:

Being Awake

*"Keep awake therefore, for you do not know on what day
your Lord is coming."*
MATTHEW 24:42

Today's Prayer

God, help me to not be distracted by the competing concerns in
my life. Cause me to be aware of what you are doing and where you
are working. Help me to do what you have asked me to, without wavering. Amen.

Today's Reflection

An interesting thing about babies is that it is difficult for them to
stay awake. When they feel tired or irritable, there is not much to
stop them from grabbing a blanket or climbing into the lap of an
awaiting parent. However, many people have long passed infancy and
adolescence and find it both difficult, if not impossible, to stay focused on God's divine plan and be acutely attentive to the movement
of God. Often a lulling complacency comes upon us and we are asleep
to the mandates of Christian confession and behavior. But Jesus reminds us that we must be prepared for the Lord's return.

My Prayer for Today:

The Smell of Victory

"But thanks be to God who always leads us in triumphal procession, and through us spreads in every place the fragrance that comes from knowing him."

2 CORINTHIANS 2:14

Today's Prayer

Loving God, you continue to be with me in hard times, in the midst of personal and corporate battles. In every situation, you consistently show me the paths to victory. Thanks for ordering my steps and for directing my path. Help me to be a reminder of your unfailing love, protection, and provision. Amen.

Today's Reflection

Sweat socks. Gold medals. Stuffy locker rooms. These are often the symbols of participation in and the markers of victory. The winner is often the one who played the hardest and lasted the longest. However, when we are in Christ, we have already joined in the winning side. Victory has been promised and the outcome has been secured. We needn't depend on any particular event, because God always leads along the path of triumph. Our faith and obedience become the witness to those who don't believe. God's favor in our lives is so pervasive that it is like the sweet smell of expensive perfume.

My Prayer for Today:

Day 126

Choosing Life

*"You are a hiding place for me; you preserve me from
trouble; you surround me with glad cries of deliverance."*

PSALM 32:7

Today's Prayer

In the midst of chaos and confusion, Dearest Lord, have mercy on
me. Even as I look upon my circumstances and surroundings, let me
know that you are near. Give me comfort and help me to be a comfort to others. Amen.

Today's Reflection

David knew what side his bread was buttered on. He had flaws,
and his personal choices often got him in hot water. But, he knew
that the best part of him was when he relied on God. David knew
that calling on God was always the right choice.

Life can be unbearable at times. Add to this our inability to lead
perfect lives, and what is unbearable becomes unlivable. A friend
once remarked that when she and her brothers were young, they
would get into trouble with their childish pranks. Their mother,
upon discovering them, would admonish them with the words, "You
better choose life." What she gave them was a choice sometimes between a spanking and straightening their act. "It was usually an easy
choice," the friend remembers.

God brings life to us daily. Choosing life is what God requires of
us.

My Prayer for Today:

Day 127

Undeserved Forgiveness

*"But Esau ran to meet him, and embraced him, and fell on
his neck and kissed him."*

GENESIS 33:4

Today's Prayer

Gracious God, I thank you for my family. Please God give me the
strength to put past hurts behind me. Give me the courage to love
those who may have wronged me. Give me an open heart to forgive
and receive them, that I may be an agent of healing. This I ask in the
name of Jesus. Amen.

Today's Reflection

You know the wounds, the painful memories, and the heartbreak
that only those we love can inflict. We ask God to give us a forgiving
heart, for in forgiving those who have wronged us we heal ourselves.
We remember what God requires of us is not judgment, blame, or
ridicule, but love. "How many times must I forgive my sibling?"
Jesus answers, "seventy times seven." Today, forgive a grudge. Today,
give that one family member who lies outside of your grace another
chance.

My Prayer for Today:

Deadly Defiance

*"But the Lord hardened Pharaoh's heart, and he would not
let the people of Israel go."*

EXODUS 11:10

Today's Prayer

Most Gracious God, I thank you for the hard places, the difficult
situations that force me to make a move. Thank you for those moments, for often, in those moments, I get a glimpse of what you
would have me do, who you would have me to be. As I go about this
day, Lord, I ask that you open my spirit to see the vision of possibility you hold for me. Amen.

Today's Reflection

Sometimes God's hand is found even in the hard places. The
places that are uncomfortable, those situations that are unjust. For
when we are between a "rock and a hard place" we are forced to
make a move. The Israelites had the option of being comfortable
with the oppression they knew, or moving on. Even with the promise
of God, it seemed an uncomfortable and frightening walk toward
freedom. Sometimes we must trust God enough to let Pharaoh go!

My Prayer for Today:

Don't Sweat

"Do not fret because of the wicked; do not be
envious of wrongdoers."

PSALM 37:1

Today's Prayer

God, I ask for patience this day. To be firm and steadfast, walking inside your will. Lord, I affirm your love, your power, and your goodness. I pray with the assurance of one who knows you are a righteous God and justice will prevail. Amen.

Today's Reflection

By all appearances, those who don't honor God, those who lie, steal, and cheat DO prosper. How do we reconcile this fact? David assures us that righteousness will be rewarded. Our charge is to trust in the Lord and not let the appearance of inequity "worry our nerves," for as the psalmist reminds us, "I have been young, and now am old, yet I have not seen the righteous forsaken nor his descendants begging bread!"

My Prayer for Today:

Staying Ready

*"Keep awake therefore, for you know neither the day
nor the hour."*
MATTHEW 25:13

Today's Prayer

Most Gracious God, give me a discerning heart that I may be
ready to serve you, ready to praise you, ready to do your will here on
earth. Save me from distractions and move me toward faithful service. This in Jesus' name I pray. Amen.

Today's Reflection

How prepared are you in your personal life? Are you always dis-
organized, always running late? How can you better prepare yourself
to meet your daily challenges? If that perfect job, that perfect mate,
or that perfect opportunity came along, would you be ready? The
same thing holds true spiritually. We must be in a constant state of
preparation: loving, learning, serving, witnessing, and praising God
so we won't be caught unprepared and left outside of God's will for us.

My Prayer for Today:

From the Get-Go

"In the beginning was the Word."
JOHN 1:1

Today's Prayer

Dear Lord, give me courage to proclaim my faith. "Let your praise continually be in my mouth." Direct my tongue. "May the words of my mouth and the meditation of my heart be acceptable to thee, Lord, my rock and my redeemer." Amen.

Today's Reflection

Words are powerful! Once something harsh or unloving is spoken it's hard to take back the hurt it's caused. John's Gospel says the Word became flesh. If your words took form, what would they look like? How would your words manifest? Would they be beautiful and flowing, or rigid with a point? Would they be warm and inviting, reverent and peaceful, or cold and hard? Speak a good word today. Think about how your words affect others today.

My Prayer for Today:

Uncovered

"But when one turns to the Lord, the veil is removed."
2 CORINTHIANS 3:16

Today's Prayer

God, I thank you for all the beauty that surrounds me: for colors soft and colors radiant, for textures jagged and smooth. Open my eyes that I can see past the mess, past the confusion, past the injustice, past the uncaring to the brilliance of your possibility. As I move through this day, help me see the certainty of your love, evidence of your power. Amen.

Today's Reflection

There are many things that veil the radical brilliance of God. What stuff is making it difficult for you to see God? What is obscuring the power of God in your life? Is it the sameness of your routine, or perhaps the limitations of tradition? Is it the weight of living in a corrupt world where disappointment, anger, resentment, or even jealousy gets in the way of you seeing God? Today, don't let your familiarity with the world block your vision of who God is and who you are. Today, look for the sacred around you.

My Prayer for Today:

Day 133

Driving or Driven

"Have you not made distinctions among yourselves . . . ?"
JAMES 2:4

Today's Prayer

God, I know you see all people as equal. Lord, keep me from seeing people only as the world sees them. Help me to see the child of God before me and not just the car someone drives, or the clothes someone wears. Help me to see the hearts of those I encounter. This I can do with your help. Amen.

Today's Reflection

First impressions impact us powerfully. We so often judge the worth of our brothers and sisters, not by who they are but by the labels on their backs, the cars they drive, their income, and even where they live. The Bible cautions us against this sin. Consider today, who and what you value, and why.

My Prayer for Today:

Day 134

Dreamers

"They said to one another, 'Here comes this dreamer.'"
GENESIS 37:19

Today's Prayer

Gracious God, creator of all things, please supply me with a vision for my life and the strength to hold on as I go through the challenges that life will present. Amen.

Today's Reflection

This particular narrative begins by telling of an already strained relationship that Joseph had with his brothers. As the narrative unfolds, God gives Joseph the gift of prophecy or vision. When Joseph begins to disclose his visions, the level of hostility within the family escalates. It peaks when Joseph discloses a vision wherein the symbols project him as being in a position of power while his family is in a position of subjugation. There are several lessons that one can learn about discretion in disclosing the revelations of God, especially when it threatens the comfort level of others. However, we learn that God's divine agenda cannot be altered!

My Prayer for Today:

Passing Over

*"The blood shall be a sign for you in the houses where you
live: when I see the blood, I will pass over you, and no
plague shall destroy you when I strike the land of Egypt."*
EXODUS 12:13

Today's Prayer

Holy God, who provides a means of salvation in troubled times, I
thank you for passing over my sins through the blood of Jesus.
Amen.

Today's Reflection

This particular account in Exodus is a story of a people who are
held in bondage. God is about to deliver them from servitude. For
the Christian community, the unblemished lamb, the blood of the
lamb, and the Passover are signs that communicate the Christ event.
They symbolize God's plan for deliverance to all humanity. The blood
of the Lamb still provides salvation.

My Prayer for Today:

Just a Visit

*"For I am your passing guest, an alien,
like all my forebears."*

PSALM 39:12

Today's Prayer

Oh Lord, help me to be as mindful of my own words as I am mindful of the words of others. Amen.

Today's Reflection

This particular psalm mirrors the movement and emotional anxiety that we all experience from time to time. Sometimes the words of others can push us to the edge. Hurtful words can cause us to doubt. The realization that life on earth is temporary and filled with pain can compel us to examine the permanence of God and the hope and expectation of better days in God's presence. Know that God's words of promise are sure and that suffering cannot endure forever. Like the psalmist, in the midst of suffering, hope and faith in God are what we have to cling to.

My Prayer for Today:

Day 137

This Is a Really Good Day

*"On that day the branch of the Lord shall be beautiful
and glorious."*
ISAIAH 4:2

Today's Prayer

Lord, help me to be cleansed of the things that are not like you.
Strengthen me that I might endure a positive change. Amen.

Today's Reflection

Oftentimes we want to move to the next stage of growth in our
lives because we believe that it will bring peace and security as well
as other good things. Much like children in elementary school, we
can't wait until promotion to the next level. But in matters of the
spirit, maturity is a process that requires the individual to address
their personal shortcomings before they can move on. The old folks
would use the term "going through the fire" to symbolize the process.
It was figurative speech to indicate the refining of gold: a process
that requires the burning off of all impurities. The process is usually
painful but the result is "beautiful and glorious."

My Prayer for Today:

Day 138

Jesus' Blood

"For this is my blood of the covenant that is poured out for
many for the forgiveness of sins."
MATTHEW 26:28

Today's Prayer

Lord of life, creator of all things, grant me knowledge and understanding of the ongoing covenant of love that you have with your
people. Amen.

Today's Reflection

The words covenant and blood highlight two of the prevailing
themes that are connected by threads of family relationships within
the Bible. The Passover was celebrated in remembrance of the covenant
that God had with God's people. The Passover was a time to remember this relationship and the blood that was shed to save the covenant
community. Jesus' words in this chapter symbolize a new covenant
with a new Passover lamb. The sacrifice that is about to take place in
this account will atone for all the sins of those who believe (see
Leviticus 17:11). There will be no need to sacrifice any more ani-
mals. In infinite wisdom, God has chosen the unblemished Lamb to
die so that we who believe might be passed over during the day of
judgment. It's not what we have done, but what God has done. Thanks
be to God.

My Prayer for Today:

Day 139

Vision Correction

*"In their case the god of this world has blinded the minds of
unbelievers, to keep them from seeing the light of the gospel
of the glory of Christ, who is the image of God."*
2 CORINTHIANS 4:4

Today's Prayer

Father in heaven, open our hearts and spirits so that we might
comprehend the eternal things of life. Amen.

Today's Reflection

The faith community within the Bible had to live in tension with
those who saw the world differently. The world has changed little in
that respect. Materialism, immediacy in results, and effective outcome models have taken root and grown in our world. What people
cling to and rely upon in times of trouble is rightfully their God. Paul
draws upon that contrast in this chapter as evidenced in the last line:
"Because we look at not what can be seen but at what cannot be
seen; for what can be seen is temporary, but what cannot be seen is
eternal." These contrasts in worldview are ever present in our Christian
reality. Where is your focus?

My Prayer for Today:

Lying Tamer

"But no one can tame the tongue—a restless evil, full of deadly poison."

JAMES 3:8

Today's Prayer

Gracious and Holy God, help me to think carefully before I speak. Amen.

Today's Reflection

Today's meditation gives one reason to be very careful in the words that one utters. The author ends this chapter by drawing a contrast between wisdom from above and earthly wisdom. Now what were you getting ready to say?

My Prayer for Today:

Day 141

Distressed but Determined

"She is more righteous than I."
GENESIS 38:26

Today's Prayer

Lord God, I give you thanks and praise for being a God of justice and love. I give you thanks for being mindful of me even when I'm not mindful of you, and for protecting me when I feel vulnerable. When all else fails and everyone has turned their backs on me, I can depend on and trust in you, O Lord. You know everything, and nothing is hidden from you. Amen.

Today's Reflection

Like Tamar, we often have done what we thought was the right thing, followed the rules, and yet found ourselves distressed and in the midst of a mess. Like Tamar, we have often trusted and believed promises, yet found ourselves betrayed.

Tamar's father-in-law knew her humiliating plight if she remained childless. He attempted to carry out the tradition in giving her his next oldest son. When that son died, he said he would give her his youngest son, but he didn't. God knows our situation and will use what was intended to be a stumbling block and turn it instead into a stepping stone.

My Prayer for Today:

Getting Home, the Long Way

*"So God led the people by the roundabout way
of the wilderness."*

EXODUS 13:18

Today's Prayer

Eternal God, show me the way that I must go to fulfill your will in my life. Help me to stay on the path you've set before me. Keep me in your loving care. I thank you for loving me and for saving me. Amen.

Today's Reflection

The children of Israel learned a lot about themselves and God. Finding the fastest way to the promised land was not the most important thing—but rather it was what they learned on the journey that was important.

The children of Israel learned that God could supply all of their needs. They worried about food, and God provided manna from heaven. Wilderness experiences are neither pleasant nor convenient. Wilderness experiences can be time-consuming and uncertain, yet priceless. We can learn so much about ourselves and our creator in the wilderness. We can see our weakness and our strength. We can see our loyalty, but most of all we can see that God is with us and that we are not by ourselves.

My Prayer for Today:

Day 143

Change of Heart

"I have told the glad news of deliverance."
PSALM 40:9

Today's Prayer

I give thanks to you, O Lord, for hearing my distress and comforting me. For hearing my joy and taking delight in it. Lord, I thank you for your unconditional love and your endless mercy that meets me at my point of need. Amen.

Today's Reflection

For many of us, a tragedy or a crisis can put us in a position of having to rely and depend on someone else. When disaster strikes and we don't know what to do or where to go, when we are overwhelmed with a sense of hopelessness, and when it seems that no one can help—at those times we turn to God as our last resort. God doesn't always change the situation, but sometimes changes us in the situation. The situation that seemed impossible or hopeless before now has possibilities and options. We thank God for the strength to go forward and not give up. We want to repay God, but God only desires from us our love and obedience.

My Prayer for Today:

Learning to Love

"He expected justice, but saw bloodshed."
ISAIAH 5:7

Today's Prayer

Merciful God, creator of every good and perfect gift, help me to be a follower of Christ. Help me to love my neighbors as you have loved me, and to treat them as I want to be treated. Keep your hedge of protection all around me. Help me to do what is required, O Lord, to walk with you. Amen.

Today's Reflection

With care we were created, and showered with unconditional love. God has supplied our every need: air, water, and food in abundance. God provides warm weather, a place to live, companionship, and surrounds us with the beauty of creation. God gives us these things freely, not because we earned them or even because we deserved them, but simply because God wants us to have them.

In response, humanity is destroying the land. We hurt one another, and charge one another ridiculously high prices for things God has freely given us. We disrespect and dishonor one another because of the color of our skin, gender, religious choices, economic status, and illnesses. If we are to walk with God, we must learn to love.

My Prayer for Today:

Day 145

Seeing Jesus

"I know who you are, the Holy One of God."
MARK 1:24

Today's Prayer

Gracious God, for your unconditional love found in Jesus, I thank you for opening my heart to understand who the Holy One of God is in my life. For it was Jesus, the healer, who touched me and made me whole. I thank you for the privilege of knowing him for myself. Bless all who call on Jesus with health and strength. Amen.

Today's Reflection

As Jesus began his public ministry, many things happened with him in the presence of others. It was very clear to all who heard and saw Jesus that there was something very special about him. When Jesus astounded and amazed people, they never once considered who he really was. Like those people, many of us are in the presence of Jesus yet do not know him. The Holy One of God is the one who loves and blesses us. He can bring joy into our lives. No matter what the problem is, Jesus can fix it. He can free us from the bondage of racism, sexism, poverty, and drugs. When Jesus touches our hearts, our lives are forever changed. He is a friend like no other. We can do all things through Christ, who strengthens us. He was the sacrifice for us and is available to us if we would only ask, believing.

My Prayer for Today:

Day 146

The Miracle of Grace

"He gave us the ministry of reconciliation."
2 CORINTHIANS 5:19

Today's Prayer

Loving God, the one who heals from the inside out. Fill me with your Holy Spirit so that I may know your love for me. Fill me with your wisdom that I might worship you in spirit and in truth. Amen.

Today's Reflection

There are many forms of human suffering. One of the most common forms of suffering is guilt—guilt that we cannot forgive long after the event itself has passed. This guilt takes on many forms, including self-indulgence, self-pity, low self-esteem, and an overwhelming sense of unworthiness. In the ministry of reconciliation, where God reconciles the world through Jesus Christ, we can overcome guilt. Jesus' way of dealing with this sense of guilt is not to excuse the wrongs; rather, through his love for us to forgive the person and to blot out those wrongs. The guilt is no longer a barrier in our lives. This is the miracle of grace, found on the cross at Calvary.

My Prayer for Today:

Day 147

Drawing Near

"Draw near to God, and He will draw near to you."
JAMES 4:8

Today's Prayer

Merciful Creator, give me a clean heart so that I might serve thee. Help me to be a light that shines in the darkness, the peacemaker in the midst of conflict, and the loving one in the midst of hatred. I thank you for molding and making me into a vessel that can be used by you. Amen.

Today's Reflection

The bottom line of the goodness is transformation, a change of mind and heart. No matter how selfish or rebellious we have been, if we repent and confess our sins before God, God will certainly answer. God will answer because God loves and cares for us. If only we would just humble ourselves, realizing that everything we have comes from God. If we submit ourselves to God, God will welcome us with open arms, embracing us with unconditional love. In good times and in bad, in sickness and in health, God loves us and blesses us.

My Prayer for Today:

God Was There

"The Lord was with him."
GENESIS 39:23

Today's Prayer

Gracious God, creator of all things, it is through difficult times that we need your blessed assurances. I pray that you would be with all who find themselves in difficult times. Use me to help others, as others have helped me. Amen.

Today's Reflection

Genesis 39 tells the reader that Joseph was "bought" from the Ishmaelites. The second and the last verse within Genesis 39 give emphasis to God's presence in the midst of situations that appear to go from bad to worse. Others influenced Joseph's condition of forced servitude to incarceration. However, Joseph controlled his attitude and the text reveals that Joseph tried to make the best of a bad situation. It also reveals that through harsh circumstances the Lord is with us.

My Prayer for Today:

In Plain View

"Israel saw the great work that the Lord did."
EXODUS 14:31

Today's Prayer

Lord God, as we go through life's transitions we pray that your saving power would be discernible to us as well as to others. Guide us in times of darkness and distress. Amen.

Today's Reflection

Exodus 14 is an account of a community in transition. The past was lived in captivity. There are several voices within the text. There are the voices of the Lord, Moses, the Egyptians, and the community. The Lord's voice reveals intention, directions, and purpose. The voice of Moses reveals encouragement. The voice of the Egyptians reveals wavering and indecision, and the voice of the people reveals protest. Often captivity can be comfortable. The people were uncomfortable with leaving captivity. Sometimes, in our spiritual lives, we too are easily seduced into captivity, but the Lord is revealing new intentions, directions, and purpose. Be encouraged. Listen and watch for the great work that God is doing for you, while you are in transition.

My Prayer for Today:

My Hope Is in God

"Hope in God; for I shall again praise him,
my help and my God."

PSALM 42: 11

Today's Prayer

My Lord and my God, it is your presence that sustains life. Please sustain me in the parched places of my journey. Allow me to drink from the well that sustains my spirit. Amen.

Today's Reflection

The voice of the psalmist is focused on memories of better times, hope for the future and questions of when, where, and why. We all go through periods in our lives when our faith is challenged. The psalm is clear evidence of our not being the only ones to have experienced this dilemma. The words express the deepest dread of the faithful—to be abandoned by God. But in the final verse of the psalm, the desperation has moved to hope: "Hope in God; for I shall again praise him." Our faith is our hope. A hope that assures us that God will not abandon us.

My Prayer for Today:

A Holy Volunteer

"Here am I; send me!"
ISAIAH 6:8

Today's Prayer

My Lord and my God, I realize that I live around and work with many who do not know of your ability to take away sin. I pray that you would use me as a vessel to deliver a message of good news. Amen.

Today's Reflection

The prophet Isaiah had a life-altering experience in the temple. His encounter with God and the heavenly host made him realize that his life, being interwoven with those around him, was not respectful of the holiness of God. "Yet my eyes have seen the King, the Lord of hosts!" Isaiah proclaimed with amazement. He was astonished in the realization that God was merciful and had provided a way for his guilt and sin to be taken away. Not only was his guilt and sin taken away, but also the Lord had sought out a messenger. Isaiah, being moved by this redeeming experience, offered himself as a vessel to deliver the Word of God. We are much like Isaiah in many ways. And God will always be God, ready to redeem us and use us as vessels for noble use. The only requirement for Isaiah was to face the truth about himself and to be willing to be used by God. The Lord still seeks out vessels. "Here am I; send me!"

My Prayer for Today:

Restored

"Son, your sins are forgiven."
MARK 2:5

Today's Prayer

Gracious God, thank you for sending Jesus to bring healing to this world. I pray thee, make me whole again through the healing power of your love that comes in Jesus Christ. Help me to know Jesus as my Lord and Savior. Amen.

Today's Reflection

Jesus came into the world to restore it to wholeness. The paralytic was one among those needing to be made whole again. He knew what it was like to live as an outsider because of his physical disability. Those who witnessed the healing realized it could only come from God. Jesus restored to wholeness one who was an outsider. Jesus had compassion on the man and made him whole again. In our world, there are many who live as outsiders. But like the paralytic, we too can be restored to wholeness in Jesus. Through a relationship with Jesus Christ, we receive access to God's healing power in our lives. It is in Jesus that we are accepted and received as children of God.

My Prayer for Today:

Day 153

Sacred Space

"For we are the temple of the living God."
2 CORINTHIANS 6:16

Today's Prayer

Lord God, I pray that the work you are doing on me, in me, and through me might be manifest in all situations. Let me be a living temple of the living God. Amen.

Today's Reflection

This portion of Paul's second letter to the Corinthians addresses the extreme ends of the conditions of life in which the servants of God find themselves. These extremes are not unique to the community of the faithful; they are a part of life's challenges to all people. However, it is our belief in God that makes us respond differently under such trying circumstances. A young man approached his minister and asked, "Why does God test me with such difficult circumstances and conditions? I thought God knew everything." The minister replied, "God does know everything. And if God is testing you, it's not to find out about you; it might be to show you things that you need to know about yourself."

My Prayer for Today:

Day 154

Weight Lifting

"The prayer of the righteous is powerful and effective."
JAMES 5:16

Today's Prayer

Lord, in a broken and ailing world, I pray for those who are sick, shut in, and less fortunate. I pray that you would heal my infirmity and shortcomings and help me so that I might not be judgmental toward others. Amen.

Today's Reflection

In our profit-oriented world, we often become blinded by what has become a common term in our daily jargon: the bottom line. This portion of James's letter begins by addressing the issue of ill-gotten gains through unjust methods and moves to ways of the prophets and the power of their prayers and ends in restoration of those who have wandered from the truth. The letter is intended for a community of believers. It is this community that is called to respond, in love, to those who have wandered away from the truth. Not only is prayer powerful and effective but so is our desire and love to save those within our community. God's desire and love for us can be shared in how we respond to others.

My Prayer for Today:

The Big Payback

*"But remember me when it is well with you; please do me
the kindness to make mention of me to Pharaoh, and so get
me out of this house."*
GENESIS 40:14

Today's Prayer

Heavenly Father, thank you for the communities that nurtured
and supported us as we grew to adulthood. Help us to replenish our
communities with all that we've received. Amen.

Today's Reflection

John-John was his pet name, but he's now called John. John is a
stockbroker, and only the twinkle in his eyes gives him away. There
are others, too—look at them now. Brian Earl is a lawyer. Little Effie
owns a big service station down the street.

Like Joseph, our parents, grandparents, and members of our communities did us a huge favor. They nurtured us. They instilled us
with values. They taught us lessons and encouraged us to be the best
in our fields. And like Joseph, they don't want much in return.
Remember them in ways such as mowing the grass or taking out the
garbage. Call and visit with them often. The best way to repay them
is to remember them in words and deeds.

My Prayer for Today:

Day 156

Praise God in Everything You Do

*"The Lord is my strength and my might, and he has
become my salvation; this is my God, and I will praise him,
my father's God, and I will exalt him."*

EXODUS 15:2

Today's Prayer

Hear me, O Lord, as I petition you to talk with me like you talked
with my parents, grandparents, and ancestors. I will sing gladly their
songs of strength and renewal. Amen.

Today's Reflection

The book of Exodus invites us to hear the freedom song. As the
children of Israel marched out of Egypt toward freedom, they knew
that their strength came from God. When we look back on our history, we see the strength of the Lord in our parents and ancestors. We
know they survived through song, praise, and worship. We saw how
God brought them through.

God lives today. When we praise and exalt God above all else, we
are renewed and strengthened for the tasks of each day. We, too,
stand on the Exodus trail of hope, for God has brought us a mighty
long way.

My Prayer for Today:

Day 157

Message in a Sunrise

"Be still, and know that I am God. I am exalted among the nations, I am exalted in the earth!"

PSALM 46:10

Today's Prayer

I am so thankful to be called yours, Lord. In the stillness, I feel your presence. In the quiet I hear your voice. Amen.

Today's Reflection

Busy, busy, busy, yet each day I found myself getting further behind. Not good. So when the call came to do a workshop in Belize, I jumped at the chance for a little relaxation. I wasn't even thinking about God.

In Belize, the nights were black and the waves were the only sound I heard. Late one evening, I walked out on the steps. I didn't know the time. I turned to the sound of the waves, and then it was there. First, an azure line. Slowly, it turned colors and for the first time I saw a sunrise like no other. In that instant, I knew the power of the Lord.

I learned that nothing is ever so important that we can't take a few moments to enjoy God's power—even in a sunrise.

My Prayer for Today:

Day 158

I Love to Tell the Stories

*"But you shall receive power when the Holy Spirit has
come upon you; and you shall be my witnesses in
Jerusalem and in all Judea and Samaria and to the end
of the earth."*

ACTS 1:8

Today's Prayer

As your wonder-working power flows through me, Lord, use me
to share this message with others. Amen.

Today's Reflection

The great writers of our time have borne witness to God's power.
From their pens we have the stories of Harriet Tubman's mission and
Martin Luther King Jr.'s dream. We witness through these writings
not only the heartache of African Americans, but their triumphs!
And it is through these triumphs that we witness the power of the
Holy Spirit that Jesus promised upon his ascension.

When we seek this power, we will be empowered by it. Embrace
it. Then we can be the witnesses for the next generations to come. It
is through God's authority alone that we are able to stand and bear
witness at all.

My Prayer for Today:

Some Rules Are Made to Be Broken

*"And he said to them, 'Is it lawful on the Sabbath to do
good or to do harm, to save life or to kill?'
But they were silent."*

MARK 3:4

Today's Prayer

If not now, Lord, when? Don't let me be swayed by unjust rules.
Help me help others now. Amen.

Today's Reflection

There were rules growing up. We always said, "Yes, ma'am and
sir," to our elders. We didn't interrupt grown folks when they were
talking, and we certainly didn't talk back to them. Those were rules
that aided in our maturity.

There were other rules. We couldn't sit at certain counters or
drink from certain fountains. We rode at the back of the bus. Someone
said, "enough." Our humanity said that we were entitled to the same
privileges white people received. It was the message Jesus gave that
day to the Pharisees. He told them that each person is entitled to
health and wholeness seven days a week, 24 hours a day. Who are
we to argue?

My Prayer for Today:

A Parent Who Understands

"For even if I made you sorry with my letter, I do not regret it (though I did regret it), for I see that that letter grieved you, though only for a while."

2 CORINTHIANS 7:8

Today's Prayer

Help me to be a good parent, Lord. It is not important that I be perfect, for perfection lies in my faith and trust in you. Just lead me so that I may lead my children in your ways and in your light. Amen.

Today's Reflection

Unlike the rap song written years ago by actor Will Smith, I wanted to be a parent who understood. Instead I found myself at odds—first with the toddlers I had and then with the adolescents they became, who made me cringe at the way they dressed, talked, and acted. We are not in a popularity contest as parents. We will say and do things that our children will find exception to. And it will hurt our hearts to have to say and do what it takes to guide our children in the ways of God. Don't fret. It may hurt, but the hurt will be far worse if you don't. In the end, facilitating our children's growth in God pays off in volumes.

My Prayer for Today:

Day 161

Time to Get It Right

*"But in these last days he has spoken to us by a Son,
whom he appointed the heir of all things,
through whom he created the world."*

HEBREWS 1:2

Today's Prayer

Help me to live this day as if it were my last, but don't let me waste one day of these end times. Amen.

Today's Reflection

Staring at the results of her medical test, the young woman saw the word she had dreaded for weeks. It was cancer. At that moment she felt such despair. What should she do now? Write her will? Tell everyone? Tell no one? Then she remembered, "I am your child." She spoke these words aloud, and they gave her comfort. Every cell in her body belonged to God, and God would not abandon or forsake her. She was going to live, and live she has. As the creator of the world, God asks us to live this life and not waste a moment of it. No matter the hour, we still have time to get it right.

My Prayer for Today:

Day 162

What Is It?

"When the Israelites saw it, they said to one another, 'What is it?' For they did not know what it was. Moses said to them, 'It is the bread that the Lord has given you to eat.' "
EXODUS 16:15

Today's Prayer

God of heaven and earth, you continue to hear the concerns of my mouth and the hushed cries of my heart. Thank you for attending to the details of my life, even those desires that others might overlook or misunderstand. Help me to recognize and appreciate your provision. Amen.

Today's Reflection

It is often easy to recognize God's provision when the divine action plan results in clearly identifiable miracles. Most Christians would agree that unexplained healing and indescribable safe passage from major accidents testify of intervention from the Deity. However, there are times when God interrupts our daily existence in ways that are suspiciously familiar, unexcitedly regular. We can desire the extraordinary and abundance and, instead, God gives daily bread and sufficiency. What we truly need may not look like anything we've ever seen before. Therefore, we need people in our lives to help us to see the miracle of the manna.

My Prayer for Today:

Gaining Wisdom

"Give me now wisdom and knowledge."
2 CHRONICLES 1:10

Today's Prayer

Gracious God, thank you for meeting every one of my needs and many of my wants. When I ask of you, you always answer me. When I need you, I find you close. When I don't know what to do, I hear you telling me which way to go and what to do. Please continue to direct, guide, and shape me. Amen.

Today's Reflection

When we were children, we were often amazed and mesmerized by the infinite power and influence of cartoon characters and fairy-tale protagonists. But as we matured, it became easier for us to believe that knowledge was found solely in books, research, and careful intellectual pursuit. That is, there was little room for information from nonscientific sources. However, King Solomon realized that it was more than common sense and scholarly study that ensured success. He rightly discerned that we must first seek God's wisdom on how to serve God's people.

My Prayer for Today:

Internal Truth

*"You desire truth in the inward being, therefore teach me
wisdom in my secret heart."*
PSALM 51:6

Today's Prayer

I confess that my self-destructive behaviors, unkind words, false
witness, and irresponsible use of the world's finite resources are not
only transgressions against my fellow humans, but also a sin against
you. When I make choices that compromise the truth, have mercy
on me. Please forgive my frailties and failures. Amen.

Today's Reflection

One expects that the proponents of education and holders of
knowledge possess a level of understanding that is founded on truth.
Scholars, professors, teachers, pastors, and activists should speak be-
yond conjecture and speculation. However, it is possible to memo-
rize facts but not allow truth to impact our behavior and influence
our choices. We can know truth and not live it. God invites us to experience truth on the inside, to be impacted and guided by a profound and deep personal encounter with the truth, who is Jesus.
Such a relationship encourages a life of faith rooted in truth.

My Prayer for Today:

A Round-Trip Religion

"Assyria will not save us; we will not ride upon horses;
we will say no more, 'Our God,' to the work of our hands.
In You the orphan finds mercy."

HOSEA 14:3

Today's Prayer

God of glory, you are so faithful in your love toward me. When I choose to stray from you, you wait for me to return. When my sins, transgressions, and iniquities seem to multiply and increase, your love and mercy abide. Thanks for always receiving me back. Amen.

Today's Reflection

Experienced airline travelers often testify to the financial benefits of purchasing a round-trip ticket. Vacations and business trips alike are less stressful when the traveler is assured that he can get back home. Likewise, our hope in God provides us with the comfort of knowing that our ultimate destiny is not limited to a non-refundable, one-way salvation that can be canceled out if we miscalculate or make a mistake. God, in Christ, has confirmed a way back to our divine destiny. Yes. Repentance is our return ticket from our side excursions on the isle of iniquity. God's unfailing mercy allows us to come home.

My Prayer for Today:

More or Less

"And he said to them, 'Pay attention to what you hear: the measure you give will be the measure you get, and still more will be given you. For to those who have, more will be given; and for those who have nothing, even what they have will be taken away.' "

MARK 4:24–25

Today's Prayer

Lord, forgive me when I hoard the gifts and talents that you have given me. Forgive me when I refuse to share my time and resources with others. Help me to see the ways and opportunities that you give me to give of myself. In Jesus' name. Amen.

Today's Reflection

Many of us find ourselves somewhere between a preoccupation with accumulating more things and a focus on saving our money and time. However, the paradox of our faith is that we gain when we give, and we lose when we save. Hence, the challenge for many Christians is not necessarily fiscal responsibility, but a sound management and accounting of how we demonstrate our faith. We must practice free giving and deep living.

My Prayer for Today:

Day 167

A Time to Finish

*"And in this matter I am giving my advice: it is appropriate
for you who began last year not only to do something but
even to desire—to do something—now finish doing it, so
that your eagerness may be matched by completing it according to your means."*

2 CORINTHIANS 8:10–11

Today's Prayer

God, I thank you for allowing me to be a part of your plan for the
transformation of my community. I praise you for inviting me to be a
laborer in the building of the kingdom. Help me to finish what I
have started for you. Amen.

Today's Reflection

It is no secret that most people in our ever expanding society are
often inundated with long to-do lists coupled with multiple assign-
ments. We must do more in increasingly shorter periods of time. Yet,
in the midst of our countless objectives, it is not unusual for us not
to find enough time to complete all that we began. And not only are
our reports or home repairs incomplete, but so are our commitments
to God and the church. The challenge is to remember what God said
to us, reflect on what we promised to God, and to begin to complete
them.

My Prayer for Today:

Day 168

Pre-Test Preparation

"Because He Himself was tested by what he suffered, he is able to help those who are being tested."
HEBREWS 2:18

Today's Prayer

God of glory, when I am overwhelmed by the situations and circumstances that surround me, help me to know that you are there with me. Remind me that while human help can fail, divine assistance is never far off. In Jesus' name. Amen.

Today's Reflection

When students take a test, they seem to score higher when the questions have been clear and the answers found in the previous class materials. Tests can be endured when the teacher has not only prepared the students through lectures, but when she or he has been diligent enough to take the exam first, to make sure that the test is doable. Likewise, Jesus endured suffering so that we might be convinced that we can, and will, be victorious in the midst of our distress. His work on Calvary reminds us that the trials in our lives are not insurmountable examinations.

My Prayer for Today:

God Provides

"The Lord said to Moses, 'Go on ahead of the people, and take some of the Elders of Israel with you, take in your hand the staff with which you struck the Nile, and go.' "
EXODUS 17:5

Today's Prayer

Most gracious and eternal God, the Exodus is the historic frame of reference for so many of us. Our freedom is rooted in your goodness and care for us. May our gratitude be as eternal as your love and our memory as sure as your promises. In the name of Jesus we pray. Amen.

Today's Reflection

A thirsty people questioned their leader, Moses, in the hardship of the wilderness. In desperation, Moses seeks the help of the Lord. God's grace is always as specific as our need. God reminds Moses that he already has what he needs: God is still with them, and the rod that struck the Nile River is still in Moses' hand. When he uses it to strike the rock, water flows readily and sufficiently. May we in our own lives witness to the sovereignty of God.

My Prayer for Today:

God's House Is Greater

"The house that I am about to build will be greater, for our God is greater than other gods."
2 CHRONICLES 2:6

Today's Prayer

O Eternal God, I read the biblical history of a people whose kings are measured by their faith in you. I am amazed at their progress. I am aware that whatever wisdom or knowledge is mine in this day in which we live is needed in building community—your kingdom. This is what Jesus taught his followers. Enable each one of us, by your Holy Spirit, to love enough to be your temples of strength and love in this needy world. Amen.

Today's Reflection

2 Chronicles continues the history of David's royal line. His son, King Solomon, is inspired to lead the people in building the great temple in Jerusalem. I reflect on his leadership and know that I am required to do more than build physical structures to the glory of God. The message of Christianity is to be used by a Great God to build relationships with people throughout the world; to contribute to a community of love that accepts all people as children of God; and to build economic systems that eradicate poverty and ensure peace.

My Prayer for Today:

Don't Be a Fool!

"Fools say in their hearts, 'There is no God.' They are corrupt, they commit abominable acts; there is no one who does good."

PSALM 53:1

Today's Prayer

Have mercy upon us, O Lord. Have mercy upon me! I seek to do good in a world where goodness is measured materialistically. I am blessed and I am grateful. Help me to understand that there are many people seeking to close the gap between those who have more than they need and those who have nothing. Let me never denounce your presence either in my heart or that of others. I know that I cannot make it, we cannot make it without you. Forgive us our godlessness and restore us to your powerful presence. Amen.

Today's Reflection

The grace note in this psalm is the expectation of God. God constantly seeks those who struggle to be faithful. "God looks down from heaven on humankind to see if there are any who are wise, who seek after God." God always expects someone to choose God's side. This is the message of the cross and the pentecostal power of the Holy Spirit. No matter how dire circumstances may be, God awaits the opening of the doors of our hearts so that God may dwell within us. I must want to be used by God to make a difference. I want you to use me, O Lord!

My Prayer for Today:

True Repentance

*"Rend your hearts and not your clothing. Return to the
Lord, Your God, for God is gracious and merciful,
slow to anger, and abounding in steadfast love,
and relents from punishing."*

JOEL 2:13

Today's Prayer

Gracious, loving God, where would I be without your love? How could I survive without your mercy? I place myself within your open arms. Equip me with the power of your Spirit so that I may be your true servant. Let your will be done in and through my life. In the name of Jesus, the Christ, I pray. Amen.

Today's Reflection

The preaching of Peter at Pentecost is so rightly set in the prophecy of Joel. The time of which the prophet speaks is being experienced. God's Spirit is being poured out on all flesh, "and your sons and your daughters shall prophesy, and young men shall see visions and old men dream dreams." The inexplicable has been explained centuries before. God is a creative God, always recreating, constantly restoring. Praise God! Praise is the only proper response. God remains faithful.

My Prayer for Today:

Day 173

Getting Clean

*"When he saw Jesus from a distance he ran and bowed
down before him and he shouted at the top of his voice,
'What have you to do with me, Jesus, Son of the Most High
God? I adjure you by God, do not torment me.' "*

MARK 5:6–7

Today's Prayer

O Gracious Master, help me to share faith in you. I know what
you have done for me, and I stand amazed in your presence. Give
your church proclamation power in these needy days. In your name
we pray. Amen.

Today's Reflection

The healing story of the man with an unclean spirit is marked
with authenticity by the one who knows who Jesus is. He knows that
Jesus can do anything because of who he is. He does not realize that
the love of Jesus will heal him, relieve him, give him new life. No
wonder he wanted to join those who followed Jesus, but Jesus refused to take him and said to him, "'Go home to your friends and tell
them how much the Lord has done for you, and what mercy the
Lord has shown you' . . . he went away, proclaiming the healing of
the Lord, and everyone was amazed!"

My Prayer for Today:

Day 174

Investing by Giving

*"You will be enriched in every way for your great generosity
which will produce thanksgiving to God through us."*
2 CORINTHIANS 9:11

Today's Prayer

Gracious God, your word holds the answers to our attitudes in
this market-conscious society. Wealth is not the answer for our hap-
piness. No amount of security can deny the violence of our society.
Open our hearts and our lives so that our knowledge may effect the
abundant life for all. In the name of Jesus, I pray. Amen.

Today's Reflection

Paul writes to the Christian community at Corinth, encouraging
them to contribute to the poorer Christian community in Jerusalem.
Those who have enough of everything are urged to freely share, ex-
pressing their own gratitude to God who has so blessed them. Paul's
teachings and writings help us to understand that belief in Jesus
Christ is best expressed in sharing with others. In God's bounty there
is enough on God's earth for all. Inequities are caused by our assumption of power! Poverty is a problem we can solve in God's world.

As medical science is advanced, treatment for illnesses is needed
by everyone. Making our technological and scientific advantage available to all and committing them to peaceful purposes demand self-
limitation on profit motives. Education is not personal choice—it is
public responsibility.

My Prayer for Today:

Listening for Jesus

"Therefore as the Holy Spirit says, 'Today if you hear his voice, do not harden your hearts as in the rebellion, as on the day of testing in the wilderness.' "
HEBREWS 3:7–8

Today's Prayer

Dear Savior, you lived in this world as a human being, subject to all the inequities of life. You chose to do the will of God, faithful unto death. Your presence with us, through the power of the Holy Spirit, still directs and guides, enables and strengthens. Forgive our weakness. Give us the will to do your will, until the day shall come when we shall see you face to face and tell the story of your amazing grace. Amen.

Today's Reflection

The life, death, and resurrection of Jesus Christ forces a shift in the paradigm of what life is all about, for believers in him. For those first-century Christians, it meant undergoing much persecution. Many of these Jewish Christians were tempted to return to Judaism. The author of Hebrews urges them in such a way that they will hold fast to their confessed belief in Jesus Christ. For them he is both sacrificial lamb and priest. The stories of the faithful ones may comfort them, but the substance of faith itself must grow weary for them as they wait for the return of Jesus. The building up of the spirits of this community of faith rests solely on their own shoulders. They, like us, became partners with Jesus Christ. The Holy Spirit bears witness that the faithful journey is not in vain. Can you hear Jesus calling you?

My Prayer for Today:

You Cannot Do It Alone

*"You will surely wear yourself out, both you and these
people with you. For the task is too heavy for you; you
cannot do it alone."*

EXODUS 18:18

Today's Prayer

Great God of liberation, you have given us much ministry to do.
Grant us wisdom to work together, to ask for help, to create community. In Jesus' name. Amen.

Today's Reflection

Fresh out of seminary, I worked with two other pastors sharing
ministry in New Jersey. Patti and John were wise counselors and
wonderful teachers. The most important lesson I learned from them
and the churches we served was the importance of teamwork.

We took turns preaching; we divided other tasks based on our
gifts. Moses' first elders came to be because a wise counselor, his
father-in-law, Jethro, recognized that Moses was on the road to burnout.
To lead God's people on his own would wear him out, and the people, too. There is so much to do in God's kingdom. We're called to
do our part. We cannot do it alone. Teams are God's gift to keep us
fresh for the journey.

My Prayer for Today:

The Church's One Foundation

*"He set up the pillars in front of the temple, one on the
right, the other on the left; the one on the right he called
Jachin, and the one on the left, Boaz."*
2 CHRONICLES 3:17

Today's Prayer

Great God, help us to build our foundation on your Word, your
strength, your peace. Through Jesus Christ. Amen.

Today's Reflection

At the annual New Church Development conferences I used to attend, seminars and conversations sometimes focused on the building
needed for the congregation. Land had to be purchased, specifications
drawn up and funding secured. It was exciting to come the next year
and hear about groundbreakings, fresh new sanctuaries where God's
praises were sung, and multiple-use spaces for ministry to the whole
person.

Solomon must have been excited building the temple of the Lord.
The account of its construction in 2 Chronicles is rich with detail
about its foundation and specifications: length and height; wood and
gold adornments; cherubim and curtains—all described so that we
can almost see it for ourselves. Solomon put two pillars in front of
the temple; their names say perhaps more about its foundation and
specifications than anything else. Jachin means "God establishes."
Boaz means "In God is strength." May God establish our foundation;
in God may we find strength.

My Prayer for Today:

Blessings Are Assured

"But surely God is my helper, the Lord is the upholder of my life."

PSALM 54:4

Today's Prayer

Holy, holy, most holy God, you are our help, our refuge, and our strength. Continue to hear and answer us, we pray. In your time. Amen.

Today's Reflection

Early childhood is such an important time in our personal and spiritual development. When we cry out of hunger or distress, the response of those who care for us shapes our outlook. When they come, we learn to trust them and our environment. With this assurance, seeds of faith are planted. We come to believe our parents are good, we are good, and the world we know is a safer place. Our faith in the goodness of God grows in this rich soil.

As we grow we learn the world is not so safe. We suffer, others suffer. We make mistakes and hurt others, and they hurt us. We cry out to God, hungering for peace and relief from our distress. God responds. God comes, like no other. In God's way and in God's time. Surely, God is our helper. God upholds our lives and calms our fears. God feeds us with the bread of life. God protects us and keeps us— rest assured.

My Prayer for Today:

Day 179

Like Shelter in a Storm

*"The Lord roars from Zion, and utters his voice from
Jerusalem, and the heavens shake. But the Lord is a refuge
for his people, a stronghold for the people of Israel."*
JOEL 3:16

Today's Prayer

Keep us safe, O Lord, our strength. Hide us in the cleft of the
rock; give us shelter from the storms of life. In Jesus' name. Amen.

Today's Reflection

Summer showers invite us to get wet. We may shed umbrellas and
turn our faces up to the rain. We feel refreshed and rejuvenated.
Summer storms are different. The wind whips and roars like an
angry lion. Lightning flashes. The earth and the heavens shake. Then
the sky splits open and water pours forth. Summer storms make us
run for shelter.

Same rain, different experience. God is like that. God is a formi-
dable enemy to the foes of God's people. Desolation and famine are
arrows in God's quiver, used to defeat wickedness. On the other
hand, God's people are nourished with sweet wine and flowing milk.

God is like a summer storm to the wicked; God is refuge and re-
freshment for his people. Let us turn our faces toward God.

My Prayer for Today:

Day 180

Time Out

*"And they went away in the boat to a deserted place
by themselves."*

MARK 6:32

Today's Prayer

Eternal God, our peace, meet us in a quiet place today. There, may
we find in you solace, and in ourselves a quiet joy. In Jesus' name.
Amen.

Today's Reflection

Most of us are so busy these days; we live by our calendars or
Palm Pilots. Without them, we are lost sheep—off-track and dis-
organized. Juggling priorities is a challenge, and oftentimes we
collapse at the end of the day, dissatisfied that we have not ac-
complished all of our objectives. How do we balance the demands of work and family? When do we find time to exercise
and play? How do we act as good stewards of God's creation, our
own time and our talents? These are questions that Christians
answer each day. If we are clever, we search the scriptures for
clues. If we are faithful, we may hear Jesus' voice giving clear
guidance. Surely we will hear Jesus telling us to go into the
world together, with very little, to teach, heal, and forgive. We
will also hear Jesus inviting us, compelling us to take a time-out.
"Come away to a deserted place all by yourselves and rest a
while," he says in verse 31. The disciples respond and do as
Jesus commands.

Jesus, a good rabbi, understood the value of Sabbath time. If it was good enough for him, perhaps we might find it of some value.

My Prayer for Today:

Bragging Rights

"Let the one who boasts boast in the Lord."
2 CORINTHIANS 10:17

Today's Prayer

Humbly we approach your throne of grace, Holy God, knowing that we stand only on you. In you, we have peace; in you we have life. Thank you for this free gift. Amen.

Today's Reflection

My brothers were all so cute when they were children. That certainly was something to brag about. Gifted, strong, charismatic, brilliant. Passionate, courageous, brave, beautiful. Patient, kind, joyful, prayerful. God has certainly bestowed gifts and blessings on us all. We can all find something to be proud of, to celebrate. When we cannot see it for ourselves, others may see it in us. But we give God the glory. For it is only in the Lord that we boast.

My Prayer for Today:

Day 182

Come Boldly

*"Let us therefore approach the throne of Grace with
boldness, so that we may receive mercy and find grace to
help in time of need."*
HEBREWS 4:16

Today's Prayer

Lord, we want to come boldly to the throne of grace. There at
your feet may we find healing and forgiveness, through Jesus Christ.
Amen.

Today's Reflection

I enjoy a nice party, I must confess. Occasionally my life is so full
that I will need some encouragement to get there. I know that I am
invited, but I need some coaching to get me moving.

"Come on, everyone will be there. I am going," a friend might say.
We have all been invited to sit at the table with our Lord, to be in
communion with the saints, to live lives free of sin. God has invited
us. And sometimes we are reluctant to get moving. There is one who
urges us to come. He is the one called Jesus. He is our high priest,
one who understands our weaknesses.

How? Well, Jesus was fully human. Fully. He understands our trials. He understands our fears and failures. Jesus is saying, "Come
boldly to that which lies before you!" Come boldly to the throne of
grace. There is peace, there is joy, there is rest.

My Prayer for Today:

Contributors

The following people wrote daily devotions for *Morning by Morning*:

Maria Alma Copeland

Alise Barrymore

Barbara Berry-Bailey

Ronald S. Bonner

Linda Boston

Diana Bradie-Timberlake

Wyvetta Bullock

Leslie Cannon

Joseph Donnella, Chaplain, Gettysburg College,
Gettysburg, Pennsylvania

Barbara Essex

Michelle Hughes-Wade

Karl Johnson

Regina Johnson

Vera Johnson

Leotyne Kelly

Walter May

P. K. McCary

Madline Sadler

Rodney Sadler

Angela Shannon

Susan Smith

Gwen Snell

Harvard Stephens

Joyce Thomas

Jacqueline Lewis Tillman